Tucker's Luck

Tucker wasn't prepared for the disastrous mess outside in the big world. He knew he'd never be a brain surgeon, but at school they'd given him to understand that things would at least be all right. Yet he was having problems in finding any kind of job at all.

Nor was Tucker prepared for the difficulties in finding a girlfriend. He reckoned he deserved the best! – yet all he seemed to end up with were ridiculous problems and unexpected complications.

What was happening? What was he doing with himself? What sort of life was he leading?

*Other titles by Jan Needle
published in Fontana Lions*

GOING OUT
GREAT DAYS AT GRANGE HILL
PIGGY IN THE MIDDLE
MY MATE SHOFIQ
ALBESON AND THE GERMANS
A SENSE OF SHAME
THE SIZE SPIES
ANOTHER FINE MESS

Other GRANGE HILL titles published in Fontana Lions

GRANGE HILL RULES O.K.? Robert Leeson
GRANGE HILL GOES WILD Robert Leeson
GRANGE HILL FOR SALE Robert Leeson
GRANGE HILL HOME AND AWAY Robert Leeson
FORTY DAYS OF TUCKER J Robert Leeson
TUCKER AND CO Phil Redmond

JAN NEEDLE

Tucker's Luck

Based on the BBC television series
TUCKER'S LUCK
by Phil Redmond

FONTANA LIONS

First published in Fontana Lions 1984
by William Collins Sons & Co Ltd,
8 Grafton Street, London W1

Copyright © Jan Needle 1984
Copyright © In the TV format Phil Redmond 1984

Printed in Great Britain
by William Collins Sons & Co Ltd, Glasgow

For Darrell, Ana, and Vanessa

Chapter One

Apart from the fact that he was skint, hungover, and womanless, Tucker Jenkins had it made. He lay in the bathwater, watching the steam making patterns in the air, and contemplated his existence. Good points first.

Good.

Points.

First.

Well, thought Tucker. Tommy could have chucked up all over my hair, I suppose, not just my jacket. Yeah.

He thought of the jacket with disgust. Ruined, probably. Well Tommy could pay to have it cleaned, in any case. The berk.

He laughed, and small waves splashed backwards and forth across his chest. What a performance! Tommy lying helplessly in someone's garden, while Tucker and Alan crashed about in the privet trying to get him on his feet. Halfway over the hedge – and wham. The technicolour yawn. Mate or no mate, that was that. They'd shoved him back into the garden and left him there. Die, you bastard! If I feel rough, thought Tucker, he must feel worse. That's something. Another good point.

Cheered, he felt about in the water until he found the soap. It was getting quite soft and soggy. He considered using it, rubbing it on the flannel and having a scrub, then dropped the idea. Too much like hard work. He wasn't dirty anyway. Let it soak away.

Tommy was a double fool for getting legless, because he'd been making progress with the best-looking girl in the place. She was only fifteen, true, and she was still at school, but she was a definite cracker. She'd danced with Tommy several times, and got quite smoochy. Then he'd become incapable and Allison Powell had left to go home with her friends. What a waste.

5

Maybe it wasn't, though. Because everybody knew that lovely as she was, Allison Powell spelled trouble. Although he hadn't been in evidence at all last night, she had a minder. Tucker scratched his nose. Allison Powell went out with a gorilla.

'Passmore,' he cried aloud, in his best theatrical voice. 'Thou shalt not have *my* bones for breakfast, thou porkpie hatted varlet. But thou shalt surely wreak thy vengeance on Sir Tommy!'

Passmore. That was the bastard's name. He was big, and mean, and nasty. A bit of a skin, with the boots and a funny little hat you never, never, *never* laughed at if you wanted your face. And bloody Tommy Watson was messing with his girl.

'Rather you than me, Sunshine,' said Tucker, wiping the sweat from his brow and licking his hand to taste the salt. 'No wonder you got drunk!'

Tucker had tried his hand with a variety of girls, and he'd got the signal from at least one of them. He knew – now – she was called Michelle, and he'd seen her around a few times. She wasn't a bad looker, although she was a trifle on the large side for Tucker, with dark smooth hair and a bold look. She was a good dancer, and there was some sort of hidden promise to her, as though she definitely might. So what was up? Why hadn't he tried to get her for the night? Why hadn't he made a date?

Tucker idly tried to turn the hot tap with his toe, but couldn't. Time to get dressed. Time to get down to the Dole House. His headache was practically gone. And today was sign-on day.

Another good point. He'd sign on the dotted line, and soon his wallet would be lined with the huge stack of cash so bountifully paid him by the Government.

'I'm Britain's future,' he told the ceiling tiles.

'And anyway,' he added, his mind reverting to Michelle. 'I don't really fancy her. I deserve – ' With an enormous slosh of water he stood up. He rubbed the mirror with his hand so that he could admire his sexy, manly form. My God, what a gift! If only they knew what they were missing!

6

'I deserve something better,' he said.

Tommy Watson could not remember much about the night before, but he guessed it must have been bad news. He'd been awoken violently at some ungodly hour by his mother, who had yelled incoherently at him for five minutes or more. Tommy had taken the line of least resistance, and apologised for anything and everything, over and over again.

Until she'd gone. To work, thank God. And left him to revert to painful unconsciousness for a couple of hours more.

While blacked out, Tommy had dreamed fitfully of Allison Powell. He'd had his eye on her for ages, ever since a disco at her school, Brookdale. She was a cut above his set, the old Grange Hill gang, and she lived in a smart, quiet street with a strict father who ran a driving school.

Properly awake at last, Tommy carried on his line of thought. He'd danced with her, and he'd snuggled up a bit, and they'd got on like a house on fire. But there were worries, nagging doubts. She was sweet and respectable, but she was a tease. She was sweet and respectable, but she went with Passmore. Her father was strict and middle class, but . . .

She went with *Passmore*!

Lying in his narrow bed, about a million feet up in a tower block of flats, Tommy Watson had a vision of hell. Passmore, with his cropped hair and his frightening, stupid, hat, came knocking on the door. His violent, sneering face glared at him.

'You've been dancing with my girl.'

'No. No I haven't. There's been a misunderstanding.'

When he was younger, Tommy used to stand on the balcony for ages, staring through the railings at the tiny picture of a busy street far, far below him. Now, he imagined what it would be like to plummet down, to whirl through the air screaming. After Passmore had picked him up and chucked him over the top.

He would, thought Tommy, desperately. He bloody would an'all!

7

So later, when he walked slowly towards Alan's house, balancing his aching head three feet above his heaving stomach, he almost jumped out of his skin when he heard Allison Powell's voice behind him in the street.

'Hello!' she called. 'It's me! What happened to you last night?'

Despite himself, Tommy felt a rush of pleasure when he turned and faced her. Allison Powell was small, and bright-faced, and vivacious. She was wearing a short skirt and a crisp white blouse. She was gorgeous.

'Oh. Hi,' he said. 'Why aren't you at school?'

Allison Powell laughed.

'After last night! You must be joking. I told my Mum I was ill.'

'Huh,' went Tommy Watson. 'I *was*. I still am. I feel like death warmed up.'

'Yeah,' she said. 'You look it! And I saved the last dance for you, as well.'

Tommy had a quick mental replay of what he'd been doing at the time of the last dance. He didn't think Allison would have enjoyed sharing that, much. He gave her a wan smile and reached for the plastic bag she was holding.

'Would carrying your bag make up for it.'

'Oh, what a gent!'

'Yuss, missis,' he croaked. 'Hennything to oblige, I'm sure. Where you going?'

'Home,' replied Allison. 'I've just been getting some shopping, that's all. Were you *really* drunk last night?'

Tommy weighed up the pros and cons. Women could be strange about things like that, especially well brought up women like Allison Powell. She might be bowled over by his devastating honesty if he told the truth. Or, on the other hand . . .

'Nah, of course I wasn't,' he lied. 'I had a bit of gutrot, that's all. You don't think I'd miss a chance to get cheek to cheek with you just for the sake of a drink, do you?'

Allison lowered her eyes demurely.

8

'Is it that important, then?'

They were crossing the road to her front door, and Tommy was walking on air. Passmore no longer existed. Passmore was a myth, a bad dream. Just say the word, Tom, he told himself, and Allison is yours. Just say the word.

'Oh,' said Allison.

She stopped, looking uncertainly up the street. Tommy followed her gaze.

Passmore did exist. He was standing under a tree not thirty feet away, looking at them coldly. He was not alone.

Passmore looked dangerous, but his mate was something else. Laughingly known around the place as Brains, he had a face like a skull, with a thin covering of shaved black stubble. To Tommy Watson's frightened eye, he appeared to be nothing but bone and boots. Knuckles, elbows, knees and forehead. Beside him, Allison muttered: 'He's not meant to be here. My Dad'd *kill* me if he –'

But Tommy wasn't listening. As Passmore and Brains sprang forward, he turned and ran.

'Tommy!' shouted Allison. 'My bag!'

Your bag, he thought. My *life*!

Tommy Watson ran like fury, but he could sense the apes behind him. When he saw a moving bus ahead he put his head down and gave it everything he'd got, Olympics fashion. When the platform was close enough he jumped for it, and clung panting to the rail. Passmore and Brains decelerated on the tarmac behind him, shouting threats.

Tommy could not listen. Suddenly last night's booze, what was left of it, decided that it wanted out. As the bus lurched round a corner, Tommy dropped his guts into the gutter.

Allison Powell went around with *that*. It was appalling.

Alan Hargreaves had had a bad night as well, although he hadn't drunk too much. Alan Hargreaves was in love, or trying to get over it, and the whole evening had been agony. Susi McMahon had been there, and she'd given

9

him the bum's rush some time ago. Trouble was, Alan could not accept it. He couldn't believe it was final. Result: torture.

When Tucker turned up to take him to the Dole, he'd just decided he needed another meal. He knew he couldn't be hungry, because he'd already had cornflakes and a pile of toast, but he needed something. He went into the kitchen and turned on the gas. Eggs, that was it. Eggs and bacon, and a piece of fried bread or three. And a nice cup of tea. He called through to his mate, who was reading the Mirror.

'D'you want some nosh, Tucker? I'm doing a fry up.'

'Jesus, Alan, aren't you scared of bursting, mate? I couldn't face nothing if you paid me.'

'Well, I've got to keep me strength up, haven't I?' said Alan. 'Are you sure?'

'Positive,' said Tucker. 'It says in the paper I'm one of the despairing millions without a job. It's obviously put me off my grub.'

'Too much booze, more like. You drink too much you do, Tucker.'

'At least I'm thin and beautiful. Seriously, Al, do you *need* more grub? It's no wonder Susi . . .'

Alan Hargreaves appeared in the kitchen doorway, podgy, pale and glowering. He held a smoking frying pan in his hand.

'Knock it off,' he said. 'You sound just like my bleeding father. What's happened between Susi and me is just a temporary thing. Mind your own business, eh?'

Tucker stared at the formica table top as Alan disappeared. Oh yeah, he thought sarcastically. Alan, boy, if only you could have seen yourself last night, fawning round her like a kicked dog. It was bloody pathetic.

Alan returned to the stove and slammed the pan down savagely. It made it worse to know that he was blushing at Tucker's remark – not just angry, but ashamed into the bargain. He knew he'd made a fool of himself, and he knew it had showed. The trouble was – what else could he do? He could not stay away from her, and he could not hide the pain. It was cutting him to pieces.

Alan sloshed fat over the two eggs and prepared to slide them onto his loaded plate. The prospect of eating the food filled him with no pleasure, but he felt hollow. It was not a hollowness that eating would sort out.

When he walked through into the inner kitchen, the dinette as it was known, Tommy Watson had just arrived. He put on a disgusted look as Alan plonked down his plate of fry and smothered it with sauce.

'Groo, Al,' he said. 'You'll make me feel dog-rough again. And I thought I'd run it off.'

'Run?' said Tucker. 'You're bent, you are, Watson. You'll have a heart attack.'

Tommy sat down and put Allison's bag on the table. He weighed the teapot.

'It wasn't choice,' he said. 'I had a little meeting with Allison Powell's ex-boyfriend.'

'Ex?' said Tucker. 'I'd double check that if I was you, son. I take it the meeting didn't take the form of a discussion on the international political situation!'

'Commonwealth Games, more like. I ran like stink and managed to grab a bus. Threw up all over a little old lady on the pavement, nearly.'

'God, Tom,' said Al, through a mouthful of bacon and egg. 'You're revolting, you are.'

'You cheeky sod! Hark who's talking!'

Tucker reached across the formica and grabbed the plastic bag. He put his hand in and felt about, with a puzzled air.

'Bloody hell, Tom.'

In his hand was a pair of silky knickers. Tommy Watson blushed.

'There's a bra as well,' said Tucker. 'What have you been up to, Casanova?'

'They're my sister's' he lied lamely. 'I was doing her a favour.'

'Do *me* a favour,' said Alan. 'You must think we was born yesterday. Debbie's only twelve.'

Tucker paraded around with the bra held up to his ribcage.

'*Very* nice,' he said. 'Allison Powell's I suppose.'

'I was carrying her bag,' said Tom. 'When Passmore fronted. I didn't stay to make a fond farewell. He had Brains with him.'

'Jesus,' said Alan. 'You are a prat, Tommy. You'll get your face kicked in.'

Tommy rubbed the silky pants to his cheek.

'Ah,' he said. 'You could be right.'

He sighed, dreamily.

'D'you know,' he said. 'I think it would be worth it.'

Chapter Two

Down at the Dole House half an hour later, Tucker Jenkins – bored with Tommy's prattling about Allison and what he'd like to do to her – switched his mind into a different gear and let his thoughts wander.

My God, he told himself. Peter Jenkins – this is your life. In ten minutes time, you'll walk up to that table, and that snooty bitch Medusa will go through her processing act as if you were a prime pea popping from the pod. She'll recognise you, just, and she'll tell you you're a nuisance, and late as usual, and she won't even give you half a smile. To her you're not a person, you're a number. And after that, the great machine will roll, and the Mother State will hit you with a cheque. It's ghastly.

Depressed, he looked at the shuffling lines of punters to left and right of him. Because he always came on the same day, once a fortnight, regular as clockwork, he knew a lot of them by sight. The weird thing was, he knew them only by sight, not to talk to. Although they were all in the same boat, they didn't get to know each other. It was as if they were in cocoons, or shells. Sometimes, one of them would disappear for a while, presumably because they'd got a job at last. But all too often they turned up again, a few weeks later, looking just the same. Or sometimes just a little worse. Tireder. More fed up. Further into the shell.

Odder still, no one ever acknowledged anybody else. There were no hellos, or nods or smiles. Week after week they stood there, sometimes side by side, as if they didn't share a language even. The only thing they shared was being on the dole. You didn't say 'Ta ta, congratulations' before a punter disappeared, because you weren't told in advance. And you didn't say 'Hello, and welcome back' when they returned. You shuffled on.

13

Tucker hated being out of work. Moving slowly forward, ignoring Tommy Watson and Alan even when they included him in the chat, he turned his mind back to an assessment of the good points in his life. Or bad. But here, it had to be the bad. There was nothing good to assess. It was poison.

Bad point Number One. Despite the fact that he could read and write, and he wasn't dim, and he was as keen as mustard when he put his mind to it – he couldn't get a job. Since leaving school he'd tried a dozen times to earn an honest crust, but it was impossible. What frightened Tucker Jenkins was the inevitability of it all. No one seemed to give a tinker's damn.

Tucker recognised quite clearly that he hadn't been the ideal scholar at Grange Hill, but he still found it puzzling that they'd never brought it home to him just what a disastrous mess it was outside, in the great big world. Careers advisers had given him advice, and teachers had told him how important it was that he get his finger out and pass exams. But the overall impression he'd got was this: Times are hard, and you shouldn't piss about. But something'll turn up, don't get suicidal. Reading between the lines, Tucker had interpreted it to mean that he'd never be a brain surgeon, but he'd be all right. He'd seen himself at twenty, say, with a Super Dream at least, if not a Kawasaki.

Super Dream! He'd had to borrow from his Mum to get a provisional licence, let alone the chance to put his bum across a saddle and learn to ride like Barry Sheene. The current price of a good second hand Kawasaki that he could legally drive was several hundred. It might as well have been a million for all the chance he'd ever have – now, or when he was twenty, or if he lived to be a thousand! Point Two – bad point: Tucker resented almost nothing on earth more than window shopping at the Kawasaki showrooms, but he couldn't stay away. He stood there with his nose pressed to the glass drooling, several times a month. It reminded him of being a kid. Hanging around the toy shop without the forty p to buy a plastic diver or a ball. It wasn't right. It wasn't fair. It wasn't bloody natural.

Why had they done it, then, he wondered? Why hadn't they brought it home to them, at school, that there was no point in anything, that when they finished they might as well give up? Why had they pretended that everything would be all right, that it would all come out in the wash? Because they were liars, or because they didn't bloody care?

But Tucker did not believe that. Some of the teachers at Grange Hill were good people, good men and women, who'd put themselves out in all sorts of ways to help. It made him smile to think of it – a rather guilty smile – because he'd given them so little in return. But that was life. He was just a stupid kid, then. It had been *their* job to persuade him.

Bad Point Three: They didn't try that hard because they didn't dare. What would have been the benefit in that? All the time Tucker and his mates thought there was something to look forward to, they'd gone along with the whole business quite happily. They'd done damn all, but they'd done it with good humour. If someone had convinced them that the end result was *this* – well what? Maybe there'd have been a riot. A constant riot. An ongoing riot situation. Grange Hill school would have exploded.

Feeling jaded, Tucker tuned into what Al and Tommy were talking about. It was jobs, and money – they'd got off birds at last. But it wasn't proper jobs, it was Alan's rotten dad and his lousy exploitation lark.

'Listen,' Alan was saying. 'I know it's not real money, Tom, but it's something. Me Dad can't pay a lot, you know he can't. He's on his own, and business is terrible. There's builders going to the wall right, left and centre.'

'Look,' replied Tommy. 'What your Dad's offering, he's not going to be one of them, is he? It's pathetic, Al. It wouldn't keep you in extra bags of chips, you greedy swine.'

Alan looked brassed off. He got fed up with references to his eating habits. Tucker helped him out with an insult.

'It wouldn't need much to keep *you* chucking up,

though, Tom! Half a bitter and you're anybody's! What's he offering, Alan? Has he upped it yet?'

'Has he balls,' said Tommy. 'It wouldn't keep a budgie in seed. He reckons – '

'Ssh!' warned Alan. He made a gesture with his shoulder towards the Social Security officials. 'Keep your trap shut, stupid.'

Tommy flushed slightly. Talking money, in Dole House, was dangerous. Whatever the boys picked up, from whatever source, they wouldn't be declaring it, that was certain.

'Well, whatever,' Tucker put in. 'I think your old man's a chancer, Alan. I think he's got his eye on a nice little source of cheap labour. If he needs men he should pay for us, not try and get us on the cheap. He's a bloody crook.'

'Just watch your mouth, Jenkins,' said Alan. 'Whatever else he may be my Dad's not a crook.'

'No,' said Tommy Watson. 'He's too mean. He couldn't bear it when it came to share-out time with the loot! He's a bleeding tightarse.'

'He's *not* a tightarse!'

Tucker laughed triumphantly.

'Why don't *you* go and work for him then, Al? Me – I'm going to get a proper job.'

The line was shuffling nearer to Box Six. Too near to carry on with talk of moonlighting. Alan smirked nastily at Tucker.

'Oh yeah, sure you are,' he said. 'Like that fiasco last week, eh? The job that never was.'

Tucker did not deign a reply, he merely sneered. He watched Medusa giving some poor girl a hard time over some extra benefit she was trying to claim, and brooded darkly about officials and officialdom. It was all down to them in the end. They didn't make the lousy policies, but they seemed happy enough screwing them into place.

Nah, he thought. Even that's not entirely fair. Medusa was a pain – although a terrific-looking one – but some of them were reasonable. The bloke in the Job Centre had been as fed up with last week's do as Tucker had. He'd been genuinely upset.

It had come about through some stupid bet. The three of them had been lounging around the JC finding nothing worth considering, and they'd started arguing about whether anybody *ever* got a job from there. He couldn't remember the details, but it had ended up with Bigmouth Jenkins betting Tommy and Alan that he could pick any card at random and get the job. A berkish thing to do, but so what? It helped to pass the time.

The card, when he looked at it, had been for a junior clerk in an architect's office – which everyone thought was even nuttier, in view of the fact that Tucker was hardly the world's snappiest dresser. But it had turned him on to the whole idea. He'd got quite excited by the prospect of actually going for the job, and impressing them, and being taken on.

Tucker had cruised up to the little fat man who ran the Centre, given him the details, and stated his intentions. The guy had given his jeans and leather jacket some heavy eye-contact, but phoned up the firm on the spot to tell them he was coming. So far so good.

The three of them had gone back to Tucker's pad, where he'd bathed, and powdered and pampered himself till he smelt like an advert for a high-class knocking shop. Then he'd produced The Big Surprise. A smart – if slightly out-of-fashion – three piece whistle. A suit.

'Gordon Bennett!' Al had said. 'I've known you since before you were out of nappies! Tell me it's not true, Tucker, tell me! Not a suit! Not yours! Not really yours!'

It was though, although he'd never actually had it on, except to try it the day it was bought. He'd got it on instructions from his Mum, poor romantic soul, to celebrate his brother's engagement. To a girl, inevitably, whose name was lost in the mists of antiquity. Naturally, knowing Tucker's kid, the engagement party had never happened – nor the engagement. The girl had found she wasn't pregnant after all, and that was that.

'Well,' said Tucker, twirling round. 'What d'you reckon, men? A little tight here and there, a little short in the leggie-poos perhaps. But adequate, more than adequate!'

17

'Bloody hell,' said Tommy Watson. 'I'm glad I'm not a girl. I'm not sure I'd be able to maintain me purity!'

'Darling – you look wonderful!' said Alan.

And when he'd got to the offices, after spending all his scratch on bus fares, the job was gone. Not only that, but it had been gone a week.

Tucker was still white-hot with rage when he'd got back to the JC. He'd stomped up to Little Fatso with the card – which had still been in the display case – and he'd only just restrained himself from jamming it down his throat.

'You fat twat,' he said. 'You don't give a monkey's, do you? You don't care a toss? Don't you know what it feels like to go up to a jumped-up little cow of a receptionist and be told politely to go and stuff yourself? Eh? Eh? Eh?'

He'd been pushing the feller in the stomach with a fist, pushing handfuls of cards at him and dropping them to the floor. Much more of it, and the police would probably have been called. But something in the guy's face made Tucker's anger fall apart. The bloke looked frightened; then – when he began to get the drift – he looked upset.

'But I phoned them up,' he said. 'You saw me. Look son, I'm really, really sorry. I phoned them up. They said to go along.'

What could Tucker do? He'd done nothing. He'd left.

Now he was in a reverie. Medusa's voice cut into it. Tommy, who'd just been processed, dug him in the ribs.

'You're on, champion,' he said. 'Make with the humility.'

There was a certain inevitability about what happened next, because Tucker was, as usual, late. He had this little fantasy that one day Medusa would smile like a human being, and excuse him, and get his card out from his box so that he could sign on with his mates, and hang the fact that he should have been there a couple of hours before them. Only a little fantasy.

Medusa was a great looker, dead class. But you couldn't fancy anyone who loved her job so much, now could you? Not *this* job. Tucker made conciliatory noises and hoped she would let it go this time. Medusa gave him her smile

18

and told him he was too late. He would have to see the supervisor.

It was almost part of the ritual that Tucker should get het up, and wave his arms about, and make too much noise. It never helped. It did not even make him feel better. Tommy and Alan dragged him away, while the supercilious Medusa composed her features into the standard look of contempt and called for the next victim.

'Will you wait for me, then?' Tucker asked his mates. 'I won't be long.'

'No way,' said Alan. 'Who says you won't? That supervisor bastard'll keep you hanging around for hours if he feels like it.'

'And then he may not let you have your bread,' Tommy added. He did a fair imitation of Medusa's voice: 'Being late, Mr Jenkins, could well lead to forfeiture of your benefit. As you are perfectly well aware.'

'I want bread from you in any case,' said Tucker. 'I nearly forgot, you bum.'

'What for? I don't owe you nothing, Tucker.'

'Oh yes you bloody do. You owe me for the cleaning of that jacket you bowked all over last night.'

'Christ!' said Tommy. 'Leave it out, Tucker. It wasn't my fault that I bowked.'

Alan and Tucker creased. Tommy went red, then laughed as well.

'All right, you tight sod,' he said. 'I'll pay you when you get it done, right?'

'Right,' said Tucker. 'I'll take it after dinner. How about the Swan, two o'clockish? If I'm through in this dump, that is. I'll lend a fiver off me Mum until me boat comes in.'

They had a deal.

Chapter Three

For a while after his mates had left, Tucker felt a lot better. It was always well to have a plan, even if it merely involved meeting up again in a couple of hours for a drink. He wondered if he would be able to bum some loot off his mother when it came to it. He owed her quite a few bob already. But he expected so.

After he'd been hanging around outside the supervisor's room for ten minutes, however, the gloomy edge that had tinged his mood all day drifted back. There were about six of them sitting or standing in the carpetted foyer, and the sense of waste began to weigh heavily on him once more. What am I *doing* with myself, he thought.

Almost desperately, Tucker searched around for something good, or different, that had happened to him lately. What sort of life have I been *leading*, he thought. I lie in bed all morning until the old lady has to practically dig me out with a spade, I wander the streets wearing out my shoeleather and my feet, I spend what little cash I've got on hangovers I don't want, I fantasise about a Kawasaki as if just thinking hard enough'll make one fall into my lap. Something's got to be *done*.

'Hello,' a voice behind him said. 'Fancy meeting you here.'

Tucker turned, and immediately the whole world brightened up. That's another thing, his mind tried to tell him: this endless chatting up of girls, most of whom you don't fancy anyway. What an awful waste of . . . But it was too late. Rationality had no chance. He fixed an enormous grin on.

'Hi,' he said. 'Who's your friend?'

Michelle appeared slightly annoyed by this, and Tucker recognised it as being hardly tactful as a greeting.

'Well come *on*, Michelle,' he said jokily. 'I ought to know her name. She's *almost* as sexy as you are.'

Michelle smiled, although her friend put on a distant, haughty look. Stuck-up cow, thought Tucker Jenkins.

'This is Mandy,' she said. 'You keep your eyes off, Jenkins. Her boyfriend's eight foot tall.'

'Oh,' said Tucker. 'Sorry I was born, I'm sure.'

'Come on,' said Mandy. 'I'm bored. Can't we find someone more interesting around? I get tired talking with children.'

'I beg your pardon,' said Tucker. 'I didn't notice you were pregnant! What are you expecting – twins or triplets?'

Michelle laughed, a rather malicious laugh. Mandy tried to look even more bored, despite the fact that she was nettled.

'Do you know any more old jokes?' she asked Tucker, witheringly. 'What a pity we haven't got time to stand around and have a laugh. Come on, Michelle.'

Tucker looked Michelle up and down boldly. He could see that she was in two minds. She was quite good looking, he decided. And she was keen. But she didn't madly turn him on, so there was nothing to lose by seeing just how far he could push it with her mate. He switched his eyes to Mandy.

'You don't have to rush,' he said, running a glance from her sulky face to her flat stomach. 'I reckon you must have at least a month to go. Stick around and enjoy yourself.'

This time Mandy was lost for an insult. Not the inventive type. Tucker grinned. Game, set and match.

'Come on, Mish,' she said angrily. 'Kindergarten's over. I'm going.'

She jerked towards the exit with her head. Michelle grabbed her arm.

'Hang about, Mand. Tucker's only joking, isn't he? He's only having a giggle.'

Mandy pulled her arm free.

'If wit was squit, he'd be constipated,' she snapped. 'I'm going. If you want to stay and make yourself look cheap that's your lookout.'

Hell, thought Tucker. She's a spiky one and no mistake.

'Temper temper,' he mocked. 'Mind you don't bring it on premature, Mand!'

21

She told him what to do in two crisp words, and did it herself. Michelle shrugged helplessly.

'Thanks, Tucker,' she said. 'You've dropped me in it now, haven't you?'

He spread his hands.

'What did I say? What did I say?'

'Oh yeah. Butter wouldn't melt, would it? Mandy's meant to be my mate you know.'

'No accounting for tastes, Mish. Look, if you're going to catch her up, you'd better go, hadn't you?'

Michelle looked down the long room. Mandy was still visible, by the double doors leading to the street.

'I think she's waiting for you,' said Tucker. 'Expecting, even!'

Michelle suddenly laughed out loud.

'You shouldn't have said that,' she told him. 'That was too near the mark, that was. She thought she was in the club last month!'

'Whoops! What, from the ten foot tall bloke?'

'Eight foot, stupid. I didn't say he was abnormal, did I!?'

'Michelle! Are you coming!'

It was a thin cry, from down the other end. At the same time, the supervisor's office opened. A secretary poked her head out, calling for Peter Jenkins.

'Hell,' said Tucker. 'Duty calls.'

'Yeah,' said Michelle. She clearly wanted something to happen. Tucker, knowing exactly what it was, did nothing. It was a new experience this, and he liked it. Normally it was blokes who had to do the asking, risk making idiots of themselves. And as it didn't matter either way, with this girl, he merely smiled encouragingly.

'Listen,' he said. 'I better go. I'm in trouble enough already.'

'Are you Peter Jenkins?' asked the secretary, impatiently.

'Yeah,' he said. 'Coming.'

Michelle was like a cat on hot bricks as he moved towards the door.

'You could ask me out, you know.'

22

Tucker grinned.

'You must be joking, Mish,' he said, indicating. 'I haven't got the time to work out details. I'll get shot.'

'Eight o'clock tonight, then? Outside Marks and Sparks? How would that suit your royal bleeding highness?'

Mandy's voice: 'Michelle!'

'Yeah,' said Tucker, disappearing through the office door. 'Why not? Eight o'clock then.'

The supervisor was surprised to see him looking so pleased with himself and confident. Tucker caught his look, and rearranged his features instantaneously. Cowed, humble and apologetic. That's how these bastards liked you. No servility – no loot.

'Now, Mr Jenkins,' said the supervisor. 'I require an explanation. It appears to me that you are treating this office as a convenience.'

No chance, thought Tucker. It's *us* who get pissed on, mate, not you.

'Oh no, sir,' he said meekly. 'I can explain, sir. It was a misunderstanding. But first I'd like to apologise.'

Yuck, he thought. The things I'll do for money . . .

Alan Hargreaves and Tommy Watson left Alan's house far more rapidly than they'd mooched in. They'd gone there after signing on to have a bit of dinner, working on the twin premises that there'd be tons of food lying about, and no Mr Hargreaves to get at them.

On the first count they were right. Tommy brewed up a pot of tea while Alan raided the fridge and larder for the makings of yet another fry-up. The pan was still nicely greasy from his second breakfast, and they'd decided to show willing by doing the washing up when they'd polished off some grub. This, Alan claimed, would be so unexpected that they'd not get into lumber for going through the kitchen like a swarm of locusts.

It was a big one, as befitted two growing boys. There was a packet of pork sausages, four rashers each, and three eggs – two for Hungry Al and one for Little Tom. There was a thick-cut sliced loaf to fry, and a tin of Italian tomatoes.

'Pity we haven't got no beans,' said Alan. 'But if you're hoping to score with Allison Powell when you take her undies back I suppose it'll be better if you're not trumping like a rancid elephant!'

When it was ready they spread themselves all over the dinette table to nosh it down, with the paper split up between them in place of conversation. Tommy, who was a betting man, had the racing pages, and Alan, who was an intellectual, got the Fosdikes and Andy Capp. In between chewing and burping they drank big mouthfuls of hot sweet tea.

It was halfway through this scene of domestic bliss that Alan's Dad turned up. Tommy stopped chewing, guilty as hell. If *his* old man caught him at this caper there'd be hell to pay. Alan didn't seem concerned, though. He finished his mouthful, swallowed, and smiled.

'Hi, Dad,' he said. 'Want a cupper? Why ain't you grafting?'

Mr Hargreaves was a jobbing builder, and he worked all the hours God sent. He was a nice sort of bloke in the general way of things, not as tubby as his son but pretty easy-going. But today, for some reason, he was in a proper mood.

'I'm not bloody grafting, son,' he said, 'because another bloody job's dropped through, that's why. And let me tell you, Sunshine, that I am *not* in the mood to see you hogging down that food. How many more times are you planning on eating today?'

Alan glanced at Tommy, colouring. Hang about, Dad, his look was saying. We've got a visitor. But his father did not care.

'I'm sick and bloody tired of you loafing round the house all day and doing nothing in return,' he said. 'Look at that table – covered in filth. And look at that sink. I've never seen a mess like it. You're an idle parasite.'

Alan tried a smile.

'Yeah, well we *was* intending to do the washing up,' he said. 'Afterwards. Wasn't we, Tom?'

Tommy nodded sheepishly. He had a piece of sausage on his fork, but he did not like to put it in his mouth.

24

'That's right,' he muttered. 'We'll clean up after, Mr. H.' He made a gesture towards his pocket. 'I could . . . I could give Al some mon – '

'Now don't you start, Tommy,' snapped Mr Hargreaves. 'I'm not bloody Scrooge you know. I don't want paying for it. I don't begrudge you a bit of nosh from time to time. It's just – '

Alan slammed his knife and fork down. His face was flushed.

'If you're not Scrooge,' he shouted, 'what the hell are you on about? Look at it, now, you've ruined dinner for us. What d'you expect Tommy to do, enjoy himself after all that crap you've said?'

'Enjoy himself!' Mr Hargreaves shouted back. 'Yes, that's all you think about, my son. Enjoying yourself. At my expense. What *I* want to know is when the reckoning comes. And who bloody pays it, eh? That's what I want to know!'

Alan was on his feet now, facing up to his father. Tommy got up also, and started slinking, half-crabwise, towards the door.

'Look,' he said. 'I better go. See you, Al. See you, Mr Hargreaves. And . . . er . . . thanks for the dinner, like.'

He broke away, glowing crimson, and scuttled through the living room for the door. He picked up Allison's plastic bag, and his jacket, on the way. As he closed the door leading to the yard, which was stacked with building gear and materials, he heard the inner door crash shut behind him. He paused, and the yard door opened. Alan burst out.

'You miserable old bastard!' he shouted back into the house. 'You can eat the rest yourself. Think of the rotten money you'll save!'

There was a muffled shout from inside. The boys exchanged glances, and headed for the gate. Within a few yards, without a word being said, they were running.

And shortly after that – *wrecking* themselves with laughter.

Later, when they'd calmed down, Tommy Watson asked Al what had been eating his old man.

'I dunno,' replied Alan. 'Must be his time of month or something. He's got this thing about me lately, it gets right on my tits. He thinks I'm a lazy idle swine who costs him a fortune for no return.'

Tommy laughed.

'Well, you do tuck away a fair amount of nosh,' he said. 'I could keep a family of four on what you tuck away.'

'Yeah,' said Al. 'Great. You've got his act off pat. Keep it up and I'll go off you, an'all.'

'Sorry. Only making after dinner smalltalk!'

'It's not as if I don't pay my way, that's what gets me. I cough up so much of me Giro I can't keep meself in beer and Y-fronts. He needs his head examining.'

'Perhaps you ought to go and work for him. Make a gesture, like.'

'Yeah,' said Alan, morosely. 'Maybe I will one day. That's not the sort of gesture he deserves, though. No way.'

Tommy Watson transferred his plastic bag from hand to hand and looked at his watch.

'Look,' he said. 'Now we've got time on our hands, why don't we drop this gear off at Allison's? Talking of Y-fronts.'

'Bloody hell,' said Alan. 'She doesn't wear 'em, does she!? Or does she buy for Passmore at the same time? Yeah – all right. No skin off, is it?'

As they wandered along in the lunchtime sun, they talked about Passmore and his mates. Tommy admitted that it worried him, Allsion going out with him and that. But what could he do? There was no accounting for the ways of women, after all.

A pause. Then, 'No,' said Alan. Miserably. 'No, they're a bloody pain, they are.'

'Anyway,' said Tommy brightly, trying to break the glaze of Susi-worship before it set. 'Passmore's not a real problem, is he? I mean, I don't think he's really likely to pour petrol over me and break my bones. It's just talk. He likes to act hard.'

'Nah,' said Al. 'You're right. He's only normal, as monsters go. He's only got one head.'

'Yeah. And bloody daft it looks, an'all, in that moronic bleeding hat. The bloke's a berk.'

The crazy thing was, that Passmore was still waiting. Whether he'd worked it out about the bag, or whether Allison had told him, he was on the lookout. He'd recruited Brains, and they'd been cruising. Round and round the haunts of wandering boys. Two corners from where Alan and Tommy were ambling, stood Brains and Passmore. Hunting.

Suddenly – across a fortunately busy road – the two pairs came face to face.

'Oh,' said Tommy Watson, flatly. 'Talk of the frigging devil.'

'Talk of bugger all,' said Alan. 'Run!'

They did. The roar from Passmore's throat carried clearly across the thundering traffic, and they were away. No time for laughter on *this* dash. This dash was for real.

They got away, but it was a close-run thing. They headed along the pavement like a pair of sprinters, with Tommy's golden curls – and Alan's gut – bouncing like an advert for the hair lacquer that turns men's heads. When they thought that Brains and Passmore were getting too close they made death-defying dashes through the traffic, then they played tag through the busy market in the hope of shaking them off.

As they raced along the shopping mall towards the cleaners they saw Tucker up ahead. Tommy tipped him the wink and Tucker got the message. A crafty leg extended from behind a rack of clothes and Brains went sprawling – and he never knew what felled him. Farther along Alan and Tommy turned at bay, and Tucker body-charged Passmore from behind into a barrowload of fruit.

Now there were traders involved, big and furious. Tucker, Alan and Tommy Watson nipped up a concrete walkway, rolling a rubbish bin back down the slope as a last deterrent. But Passmore and Brains had other worries. Two minutes on, and it was clear that the chase was over.

27

The three of them stopped, panting and exhilarated, in the shade of a big, leafy tree.

'Christ,' said Al, at last. 'So much for normality. That . . . bloke . . . is . . . off . . . his . . . trike. He's frigging mental.'

'And I only walked her *home*,' said Tom. 'I only had a dance or two and walked home with her *shopping*.'

'Well I hope you've learned your lesson,' said Tucker. 'Next time you see her, I hope you run a mile.'

Tommy hugged the carrier bag to his chest. He grinned.

'Yes, Mum,' he said. 'I'll do my level best.'

Like hell!

Chapter Four

One peculiar by-product of unemployment, Tucker
Jenkins mused, was the unnatural cleanliness of it all.
When he'd been at school he'd been a dirty little git,
who'd gone to extraordinary lengths in the normal way of
things to avoid a wash, let alone a bath. Swimming was all
right, and it was the only time he could be guaranteed to
be squeaky-clean, after a session in the pool. But even
then he'd avoided getting underneath a shower afterwards.

Now here he was in the bath again, for the second time
that day, and about the third in the last twenty four hours.
Well it kept him off the streets, didn't it? And it was warm
and comfortable. And it didn't cost a lot. And anyway –
you never knew your luck!

Tucker did not know his luck, but he had a fair idea it
wasn't all that good. Tonight – in less than an hour in fact
– he was meeting Michelle. He was in the bath, no longer
womanless and no longer hungover. But still skint. As
skint as skint could be. He didn't even have two pound
notes to rub together for the heat.

Over tea, Tucker had tried it on his mother, and they'd
had a row. Well – an altercation. A disagreement. A non-
meeting of the minds. He'd asked her for a loan and she'd
told him nix. He'd blustered and it had gone to double-
nix. He'd wheedled and she'd spurned him cruelly. She'd
laughed in his face. Tucker had retreated to the bathroom
to lick his wounds, and because he knew it got up her
nose, the fact that no one else could use it for hours on
end. And because – he told himself again – you never
knew your luck.

Well, he thought, as he dried and pampered his manly
form, what *were* the chances? On a first date, even with a
girl like Mish, not very high. He grinned, aware of what
the lady teachers at Grange Hill who'd tried to educate

the lads about the wilder shores of sexism would have made of that. 'Even with a girl like Mish'! What exactly did he think he meant?

Tucker wasn't sure, but he pondered on it as he polished up his armpits with Brut and dabbed some toilet water round his useful bits just in case. She was a bold-eyed piece, who'd made the running all the way. He wasn't used to that, and it excited him, but made him scared as well. What would he do if she carried *on* like that? If she took the running ten steps further on? If she got him to the stage where all this preparation was called upon to be deployed, not just thought about? What if she *did?*

He swallowed, sloshing a superabundance of toilet water on, almost in desperation. Ouch! That stung. Tucker winced, then relaxed. Bullshit. It wasn't going to happen. It never bloody did . . . For starters, where were they going to go? What were they going to do? Have it off on the pavement? Buy themselves a bottle of pale to share, and get roaring drunk and totally abandoned? Face it, Tucker, he said aloud. You're broke. Wide open. If you had a jot of sense you'd go sick. This will be disastrous.

And you don't . . . do you . . . do you *really* want all this? Do you fancy her? Or is it just . . .?

He burst out of the bathroom in a rush of vapour, whistling noisily to cover his confusion. He flung his clothes on almost angrily. This was stupid. This was one ridiculous way to start an evening. Or a relationship.

Nevertheless, Tucker got to Marks and Sparks at least ten minutes early. In the warm, pleasant summer air he hopped from one foot to another, glancing at his watch, then at the passers-by. He felt half-stupid, half-exposed. But excited; somewhere in there was excitement, too. As zero hour approached, be became apprehensive. And by one minute past the witching hour, he was convinced. She wasn't coming anyway. It had all been some obscure, stupid, joke. Michelle had stood him up.

It was five past eight when she arrived, and she arrived quietly, and from the rear. The first thing Tucker knew, she was blowing in his ear, gently. He almost jumped underneath a bus.

'Jesus, Mish! Don't *do* that!'

Her smile was a challenge.

'Why not, Mr Jenkins? If you won't sweep me off my feet why shouldn't I sweep you off yours? The art of romance isn't dead, surely?'

Michelle looked great, so Tucker looked at her. It was a damn sight easier than to answer – she seemed to know a set of rules he'd never heard of. She was wearing jeans, he noted. Stretch jeans, tight and sexy, but still jeans. He knew the real rules well enough to understand that message, and it was rather comforting. A skirt on a first date, plus her come-on-let's-get-down-to-it line of chat, and he'd have been petrified! She was wearing a thick white jumper, that softened her figure while showing it off. Mm, thought Tucker. You're very well stacked, I must say.

'I thought you wasn't coming,' he said. 'You startled me, that's all.'

'Not coming! Bloody hell, I couldn't have been *nearer* dead on time, could I? Where we going?'

'Oh,' said Tucker. There was something about this girl that made him nervy. She didn't beat about the bush like others did. She didn't give him time to get his he-man act together. He thought about his pockets. About sixty pence.

'It's a nice night,' he said. 'How about a little walk? Do you like walking?'

Michelle had an oval face, smooth and open, with her dark hair drawn back so that it was also smooth. It was not the sort of face you could tell lies with, very well. It gave the game away by its frankness. She looked pissed off.

'Oh yeah,' she said. 'I can't get enough of it. The sweet smell of new-mown grass drifting off the meadows, the gentle lapping of the river as it chuckles its way down to the distant sea, the mountains silhouetted against the starlit sky.'

Tucker attempted a small laugh, a tribute to her wit. Michelle's tone hardened.

'The smell of fish and chips and dogshit, the sound of bus engines, the silhouette of – Come off it, Tucker. This is London we're in. Anyway, I've left me green wellies back at the shooting lodge. I'd get cow muck on me slingbacks.'

Tucker was speechless. He was at a loss. His mind flashed back to all that time he'd spent on bath and beautification. He'd have been better off learning karate. She was a bloody Amazon!

'Well, there is the park,' he said.

'Look, Tucker,' said Michelle, evenly. 'This is our first time out, right? When we've been going out for a while, if things work out, I expect the park will seem a very attractive place. It's dark, and quiet, and lonely. There's all sorts of things you can get up to in the park on a summer's night, as we both very well know. But I am *not* going to no bleeding park tonight. Just what do you take me for? Come *on*. Let's push off from here in any case. I'm fed up standing still.'

As they moved off down the shopping mall, Tucker racked his brains. Sixty pence wouldn't even buy them one pint, let alone one apiece. Not that Michelle would drink pints, any more than he would cocktails! He felt a complete twit. He wished he could be anywhere except here, with her. For the first time ever, with a girl on a date, he felt as if he'd lost control. He'd never *had* control. He was being walked all over. She's just like Trisha Yates, he thought. Without the saving graces.

Well bugger it. What was the point in pretending? Who was he trying to kid? Or even impress? If she liked tough talking – he could do it too.

'I'm skint,' he said. 'I'd have thought you could've read the symptoms. I've got sixty poxing pee between me and the workhouse. And my bank manager is unprepared at this juncture to increase my overdraft facilities beyond three hundred thousand. I can't take you anywhere.'

Michelle chucked her head back and hooted. She put her arm round Tucker and gave him a smacker on the ear.

'You bloody moron,' she said. 'What are you doing taking me out then?'

Tucker stopped walking as if he'd been struck by lightning. Michelle stumbled on her heels and almost fell into the gutter.

'You cheeky sod!' he said. 'As I recall it, it was *you* that asked *me* out in the first place!'

'That's right,' she said. 'But if you didn't have the readies, you only had to say so, didn't you? Haven't you ever heard of Women's Lib, Tucker? What's wrong with me asking you out if I fancy you? The way you faff about we'd never have got anywhere, would we?'

They carried on walking in silence for a while. Tucker just didn't know where he was. At last he said: 'Well, what *shall* we do, then? Whether I should have taken up your kind offer or not I did, right? And I'm skint. So where do we go from here?'

They were well off the beaten track, in a deserted, tree-lined avenue. It was dark, they were between street-lights, widely spaced. The constant noise of London's traffic was only a dull background roar. Michelle stopped Tucker and stood in front of him. She moved in close, so that he could feel her all the way down his body, from his chest to his knees. It was worth the feel.

'Perhaps it'll have to be the park after all,' she said. She moved her head forward to kiss him. Tucker stiffened slightly, then relaxed as her tongue pushed into his mouth. They stayed like that for a long time. Somehow or other, his doubts were melting away.

'Ooh,' said Michelle, huskily. 'You do that good. Perhaps after the park I could see my way to buying you a drink. Just this once, like.'

Tucker said nothing. He pulled her head towards his mouth.

'Tucker?' said Michelle, before they kissed. 'You do *want* to go out with me, don't you? I mean, with me doing the asking, and that? I mean –'

'Yeah,' said Tucker. 'Don't talk with my mouth full.'

As they went into another long clinch, he wondered for a moment or two. Did he? He wasn't completely sure. But Jesus, *this* was all right. And you had to be polite, didn't you? He closed his eyes and switched his brain off. *This* was excellent.

In a cafe not so far away, Allison Powell was also suffering from confusion, which unlike Tucker's had been going on in various forms for quite a while. She sat at the formica table, playing with a small pile of spilled sugar with her finger tip, and glancing from time to time at the counter.

Ralph Passmore was tall, and from behind he looked extremely good. He had broad shoulders, and a long back, and a terrific behind. Even doing something totally unphysical, like standing waiting to be served with two more coffees, he had something. There was suppressed energy there, and power, and physicality.

Allison bit her lip. That broad back was clad in a shirt, and framed in narrow braces. On the close-cropped, almost shaven head, was perched the little pork-pie hat. Ralph Passmore was a skin, the sort of bloke that adults feared and hated, and crossed the street to avoid. What, they wondered when they saw them as a couple, did she possibly see in him?

It was not only people in the street. Allison wondered it herself, quite often. And her father, when *he'd* seen them, had really put her through it, later on, at home. She was a respectable girl, and intelligent, and studying for her O-levels. How could she do this to herself? How could she risk it? Ralph Passmore was a thug!

Ralph Passmore returned to the table, smiling.

'There you go,' he said, putting down the coffees. 'Put hairs on your chest.'

They drank in silence for a moment or two, with Passmore's eyes always on her face. Allison glanced up from time to time, smiling shyly. This was their first time together for a while. It had been all over. She'd told him a hundred times. But he wouldn't take no for an answer. And Allison could not keep away.

'Come on, Jailbait,' he said. 'A penny for your thoughts. I've never known you so quiet.'

Allison giggled. She loved it when he joked, because she found him so funny. Jailbait was one of his pet names for her – and like everything else about him it was scurrilous.

'Oh Ralph,' she said. 'I don't know. *You* know. I'm worried. I'm mixed up.'

He took a sip of coffee.

34

'You shouldn't be,' he said. 'You should just relax, Alli. You should do what you want to do, not what your father says. I've missed you. You've got to go on seeing me.'

For Passmore, it was a long speech. Allison sighed.

'If only it was always like this, though, Ralph. You were mean to me last week. You boss me around. I'm only fifteen, I've got to do my work. I can't go with only you. I've got to have my other friends as well.'

A shadow passed across his face and Allison went tense. One of the awful things about Ralph Passmore was his moods. They changed like wildfire. It frightened her. But this time he remained quite genial.

'You sound like your father, Alli,' he said. 'But I don't mind you having other friends. It's other blokes that I can't stand.'

'Well there aren't any,' said Allison. 'I don't know any other blokes. I don't *fancy* any other blokes. It's just . . . it's just – I've not got to get involved. I've got to keep working, I've not got to get upset. I've got exams to do. It's *important*. I want to get *on*.'

It was silly, and she knew it. Sitting opposite a boy with rebel written all over him. And her a perfect model schoolgirl, middle class and on the way up. She could see why it drove her father mad.

'There isn't anyone else, honestly,' she said. 'I didn't say I didn't want to see you because of that. It's the other things. I'm too young. I'm . . . jailbait!'

Ralph Passmore leaned across the table and took her by the hands. He looked into her eyes. His face was handsome, and volatile, with the stamp of dissatisfaction and rebellion round the eyes.

'You're safe with me,' he said. 'You know you are, don't you? All joking apart. I respect you, Allison.'

She nodded. She leaned across the table and kissed him lightly on the mouth.

'Yes,' she said. 'I know I am. I trust you, Ralph. I like you a lot. I – I like you a lot.'

They drew apart, sat back in their chairs, with Allison slightly breathless. Ralph Passmore spoke.

'So if you're going out with me again,' he said. 'What about that little wanker Whatsisname?'

His tone had changed. His face had altered, also. An empty feeling swept through Allison.

'What Whatsisname? Who are you talking about?'

Passmore pushed his frame across the table now, rather than leaning.

'Bloody Tommy Watson,' he said. 'I hear you danced with him. Or have you forgotten *that* already? It *was* only yesterday, you know.'

Allison swallowed.

'I danced with lots of boys,' she said. 'It's a free country, isn't it? You weren't there, remember? And you do *not* own me.'

'If you're going out with me,' he said. 'I do. In certain ways. If you're going out with me, you don't dance with other blokes, all right? Because if you do . . .'

'If I do, *what?*' hissed Allison. She was trying to keep their voices down, trying to avoid the other people hearing. Oh *why* did he go like this? 'I've told you, Ralph, you don't own me. I'm too young to get tied down. You're doing it, you see. You're being horrible. And you were so nice. Oh Ralph, you can be so *nice.*'

Brains would have to come in then. It just had to happen. Allison saw Passmore's eyes look past her, over her shoulder, and she turned her head. Brains, the walking skull, was approaching. Passmore raised his voice.

'Because if you do, you slag,' he said. 'I'll mash your bloody face up, right?'

Allison stood up. Her chair fell behind her with a bang.

'You bastard,' she said. 'How . . . how . . . You lousy *bastard.*'

'Oh piss off,' said Passmore. He said it casually, almost nonchalantly, a throwaway line for the benefit of Brains. He smiled at Brains, who nodded back.

'Hi, Chief,' he drawled. 'What's eating the little lady?'

Allison darted him a look of hatred and humiliation. She swept up her bag and jacket and made for the door. Every last person in the cafe was staring at her, at the three of them. As she stormed out she heard Ralph shout:

36

'And if you see that poofter Watson, tell him I'll kick his head in. If you so much as look at him, the same goes for you. Right!'

When she had gone, Passmore looked balefully around the room. Eyes dropped to plates. There was a clattering of knives and forks.

'That's better, pigs,' he said. 'Get back to your troughs, the lot of you. And keep your bloody eyes to yourselves.'

'I think I'll have a cup of coffee, Boss,' said Brains. 'Had a good evening, have you?'

Half an hour later, Allison met Alan and Tommy in the street. They were near her house, on the QV for Passmore, with the trusty plastic bag still ready to return. When they saw her coming, they did a careful recce in every possible direction to make sure it wasn't an ambush.

'Hi,' said Tommy. 'What a coincidence! Do you come here often?'

Allison had walked the first flush of her rage off. It had been a good thing after all, she'd decided. It was a clean break at last. Even Passmore would not expect her to talk to him again after that. Not ever. The cheeky, foul, *bastard*.

'I only live here,' she replied. 'As if you didn't know. What do you want? Hi, Alan.'

'Hi.'

'Well,' said Tommy. 'How about a date?'

He said it jokily, and a refusal sprang to Allison's lips. But she caught it before it emerged. Yeah, she thought. I'll show that pig. I'll stick the knife in till he *squeaks*.

'Why not?' she said. She smiled sweetly. 'How about tomorrow night?'

An expression of absurd pleasure spread over Tommy's face. Allison felt a twinge of guilt. Ow! What if Passmore meant it? What if it led to . . . ow! But she crushed it down. Oh come on. He was only a feller, not a psychopath.

'Great!' said Tommy. 'Hey, Alli, that's fantastic.'

Allison, flustered, decided to escape.

'Fine,' she said. 'Now, for God's sake let me go before my old man calls the police. He was expecting me hours ago.'

Yeah,' said Tom, moving aside. 'Yes, of course. Seven thirty, then? Outside Macdonald's? I'll treat you to a burger if you like.'

'Lovely,' said Allison. 'Seven thirty. Bye!'

She had gone fifty yards before Alan nudged Tommy.

'The bag, you fool!'

'Oh shit!' said Tommy. 'Allison!' he yelled. 'Alli!'

She turned. A cluster of people were walking past, some of them her neighbours. Tommy was swinging the bag about.

'Your knickers!' he shouted. 'I forgot to give your knickers back!'

Oh wonderful, thought Allison, terrific.

Aren't men incredible . . .

Chapter Five

Even laughing with Tommy over the knickers thing, standing in the street that evening, Alan Hargreaves had a nasty feeling in the bottom of his stomach. As they walked away, Tommy elated, cockahoop, over the flaming moon, he began to get depressed. First Tucker – for he'd told them all about his animal magnetism, that had led Michelle to proposition him at the Dole – and now Watson. Al refused the offer of a drink, and mooched off home, much earlier than usual. He was beginning to turn into a gooseberry. He was the only one alone.

As his mates' relationships developed over the days, Alan began to feel more and more isolated and miserable. He knew he could still go about with them in the daytime, that was no problem at all. And in the evenings, for that matter – no one ever told him to get lost. But he felt a berk, a failure, a huge and unattractive pudding.

Inevitably, Alan's tortured thoughts kept swinging back to Susi. They'd gone out for a good long while, for ages, and it had always seemed too good to be true, somehow. Let's face it, she was cracking looking. And he was . . . what? Alan did not need to take his clothes off and study himself in a mirror to know the answer to that. He was bloody gross. He didn't dress well, either – he couldn't see the point. He slopped about in jeans and tee shirts and trainers. He was a mess. But that hadn't made it any less painful, and any less a shock, when Susi had given him the rush.

Alan, sitting over breakfast one morning, shovelling down his third big plate of cereal, winced to even think of it in those terms. Because she hadn't actually done that. She'd never told him it was finished. She'd never told him to sod off. She'd eased him out. She'd not been available. She'd been busy. For a short while he'd believed her, until the penny had begun to drop. Even now, weeks afterwards, he couldn't quite believe it.

Even though he'd seen her out with other guys. Even though she wouldn't answer the phone to him. He found himself humming the Beatles song, slightly adapted, as a spoonful of cornflakes hovered in the air, forgotten. Because she used to love me. But it's all over now.

Maybe she'll change her mind, he thought. Maybe it's just a phase she's going through. Maybe I'll try and see her just one more time. Just once. Oh Christ. I love her.

His father bustled into the dinette, his hands and forearms white with cement dust. He looked at his son with an unfriendly expression on his face. His normal expression, these days.

'Are you still eating, Fatso?' he said. 'It's no wonder your mates pull all the birds and leave you standing. I suppose it's no use asking you to give me a hand shifting this lot, is it?'

For a moment, Alan felt like screaming with anger. Or maybe bursting into tears. He liked his Dad, he bloody loved him. And he was treating him like shit. Always. All the time. Then something different happened. The anger went away. Alan dropped his spoon into the cornflakes with a milky splash. He stood up.

'Yeah, I'll help you, Dad,' he said. 'What are you offering?'

'You cheeky git,' his father began. 'Do you begrudge – '

'No, no!' said Alan. 'I'm serious. I want to start. I want to work for you, like you're always bleeding moaning on about.'

His father's face cracked into a smile.

'Jesus Christ,' he said. 'Give me a chair, somebody! Me heart won't stand it.' A suspicious look flitted across his features. 'Not full time, though? You don't expect me – '

'No. Part time. Just for pocket money. Like you want, you stingy old bastard. You've driven me into it.'

'Well,' said Mr Hargreaves. 'Alan. You surprise me. At bloody last.'

He walked over to his son and put a hand upon his shoulder. He shook his hand, warmly.

'Leave it out, Dad!' protested Alan. He went bright red. He was embarrassed.

But chuffed as well. Definitely.

Tucker Jenkins was driven into working for Mr H by two things. The real love in his life – and Michelle.

The real love in his life was lean, hard, fast, and incredibly beautiful. As he gazed through the showroom window at it he had a mental picture of the price tag. Even the deposit was beyond his wildest dreams. It was incredibly beautiful, and incredibly expensive. A Kawasaki GPZ1000. The ultimate.

Tucker forced himself to turn away, and slouched off in the thin drizzle that was falling. He thrust his hands deep into his pockets, and felt the balled-up paper underneath his handkerchief. Six quid. Six lousy greenbacks. And the fight he'd put up to get that had exhausted and depressed him. He and his mother had seriously fallen out.

Funny. Stupid. Insane. He'd ended up with six quid and a headache, when he'd started off the conversation in the hope of borrowing about a hundred. A pretty feeble hope, admitted, but it had to be attempted. Tucker was desperate.

All right, he thought, as he hugged the walls to avoid as much falling moisture as he could, all right. I'm prepared to grant I'll never get a Kawasaki. I'm prepared to accept that fantasy has got to finish somewhere. But a bike I must have. A bike I *will*. Now Mervyn's got the bike, and I've got to get the cash. And this time I do *not* need riches beyond the dreams of avarice. Or even Aberystwyth!

Merve the Swerve was one of the local bikers who'd been a mate of Tucker's brother, way back. Like most of the bike gang he was a nutter, and like a lot of them he was probably a crook. But where most of them had grown out of it, drifted on to other things, given up the filthy leathers and moved into semis call Dungangbangin with their wives and little kiddiewinks, Merve had remained true to the stink of Mobil R and the poetry of piston rods. He made a living in obscure ways, and one of them was shifting bikes. If it was not completely legal, it was good enough: he sold them complete with documents. Which was more than half the battle.

Now Merve, being steeped in biker-lore up to his unwashed neckrag, could smell a young hopeful a mile off. And he'd let it be known to Tucker, three days before, that he had a dilly. A pip. A lovely little darling two-stroke that was going for a song and went like a bird. An East European job which it would break his heart to part with for a ton.

Tucker didn't want an East European job – they hardly had the same mystique as a Kawasaki – and he knew in his heart of hearts that it would be a dog. But he could not resist going with Merve to his grubby little garage in the flats to look. Merve had sold his brother a couple of machines over the years, and apart from little matters like oil leaks and balding tyres, they had not been bad. They'd run. And beggars could not call all the shots, now could they? Or any of them, even . . .

The bike was old, and black, and *very* Iron Curtain. It was about as classy as a pair of bottle-green flares with snot stains and turn-ups. Tucker walked around it with a look of complete disdain glued carefully to his face. Which Merve could see through like a plate-glass window.

'She's a lovely little runner,' he said. 'It's a shame to part with her.'

'It's a bit old,' said Tucker, trying to sound disgusted. 'Does it run on petrol, or firewood and coal?'

'Old my arse,' said Merve. 'It's like a woman, that machine. Or a bottle of good champagne. It's improved with age. Listen.'

He pushed it off its stand, switched on the ignition and gave it one hard kick. The garage filled with the popping rattle of a two-stroke and clouds of oil-laden smoke. Tucker breathed in deeply. It was heady perfume to him: glorious.

'Starts all right,' he said. He tried to sound calm, but desire and excitement were ruining his act. He had to have it. It was his. It was in his grasp. Merve the Swerve switched off the engine.

'Course it does,' he said. 'I don't sell no rubbish to my mates. We had some good times, me and your kid. It's a little darling.'

Tucker looked at the bike with longing. He wanted to reach out and pat the tank.

'A ton, you said? I can't afford it, Merve. Honest, mate. It's just too much. I mean – it's only a rough old . . . a ton's too much.'

'Suit yourself,' said Mervyn. 'You don't buy it, Jenk, and some other bugger will. You're off your perch, you are, mate. I could get one-fifty if I could be bothered to put an advert in.'

He gestured to a cluttered bench.

'There's a crash helmet,' he said. 'A couple if you want 'em. One for you and one for the lady of your dreams. The tarts go wild for men on bikes, Tucker. You'll have crumpet falling over you.'

'Yeah,' said Tucker, too full of bike to listen to the sales pitch. 'Look – let's have a go and I'll make me mind up. Take me for a little spin.'

'Bollocks,' said Merve the Swerve good-naturedly. He was an expert in buyer-psychology. He knew his victim was panting with desire. That was a state of affairs worth money in the bank. 'Come off it, Jenkins. No deal, no drive. You give it to me definite, and we'll consider it.'

'I . . .' began Tucker. He damn nearly committed himself there and then. But self-preservation saved the day. If he welshed on Merve he'd end up with a lot of trouble; and probably no teeth. 'I'll let you know,' he said.

'No rush,' said Mervyn. 'It'll keep a day or two if you're lucky. I've only told a few people so far, as you're a friend. But don't push it too hard, kid. It won't be here for ever.'

Tucker looked downcast, and he wasn't putting on an act. Suddenly, Merve the Swerve let out a loud laugh. He was a realist, and he knew how much the bike was really worth. He could also see a disappearing sale.

'Jesus, Jenk!' he said. 'You should see your face! I tell you what, kid, I'll cut me own throat. You look the sort who'd bother with insurance and balls like that. You'll need at least a ton. I'll give the bloody thing away. You can have it for eighty.'

And when Tucker had put it to his mother, she'd gone bananas. The six quid that he'd bummed tonight would be the last. She swore it. If he did not pay her some money back, and soon, there would be trouble. If he wanted any more – and especially if he was going to talk utter rubbish about buying motorbikes – then things would have to change. He'd have to get a job, or he'd have to stay at home for a month and save his Giro cash. She'd had enough.

Michelle was waiting, as arranged, in the doorway of Burtons. It was warm despite the rain, and she was wearing a short cotton dress and carrying an umbrella. She had terrific legs, and a great figure, and she smiled a big warm smile when she saw him. But Tucker had a vaguely sinking feeling. In this weather, he was certain, Michelle would not be walking in the park. By bedtime, that six quid would be no more.

'Hi,' she said. 'You look like a drowned rat. Give us a kiss.'

Tucker opened his jacket so that he could get a dry part – his chest – against her, and they kissed.

'Let's have a drink,' he said. 'I'm going to buy a bike. No stupid! A motorbike!'

They were laughing when they got into the pub, but Tucker felt the sinking in the stomach again when Michelle ordered. A brandy and dry ginger. He ordered a half of bitter to balance the astronomy of the cost.

'I'm saving up,' he said defensively. 'I got to raise a hundred quid.'

He told her all about the bike, but Michelle was sceptical.

'Look, Tucker,' she said. 'You haven't even got enough cash to take me out. How can you afford a bike?'

He got more defensive still. They hadn't actually rowed about money, but it was a constant nag. Michelle thought life was to be lived. She liked good things. She wanted

Tucker to treat her right, which meant drinks, and burgers, and discos and the movies.

'What do you mean?' he asked. 'I'm taking you out now, aren't I? You're drinking brandy. Isn't that good enough for you or do you want a double port in it, as well?'

'Well,' she said. 'I wouldn't say no! No, but you know what I mean. You're not exactly Rockefeller, are you?'

Tucker sighed.

'I can't help it if I'm on the dole,' he said. 'And I owe me Mum, don't I? I owe her for me keep, I owe her for my driving licence, I owe her for me clothing club – '

Michelle pretended to splutter in her drink.

'Clothing club! Pull the other one, Tucker. You've got a credit account at the Oxfam shop, everyone knows that!'

'Yeah,' said Tucker. 'That's all very well, but I *did* buy some gear once. And I still owe for it, don't I? That's the trouble with the never-never. You never-never clear your debts.'

'And now it's going to be a motorbike. You live in never-never *land*, Peter Jenkins. They ought to call you Peter Pan.'

They sipped their drinks in silence for a while. Then Tucker said cautiously: 'You're hot enough on Women's Lib and that, Mish. Have you ever thought of taking *me* out for the night? Or isn't that in the rules?'

Michelle looked at him dangerously. She makes the rules up as she goes along, thought Tucker. I'm on a hiding here. A hiding to nothing.

'I pay me Mum and Dad for board and keep,' she said calmly. 'I put some money by regular, every week, I've got the future to think about. And you may not have noticed it, but I like to keep looking good. I get my hair done. I keep my face nice. And I wear good clothes. *You* get the benefit of that. But I do *not* believe a woman should kowtow to a man. *Or* buy his bloody beer.'

Tucker finished his. He thought her logic was probably suspect, not to say downright bent. But he wasn't going to argue.

'Peter,' she said. 'We've got to get jobs. I'm up to here with this. We've got to get our fingers out and look. You make me sound like a hard bitch but I'm not. We can't waste our lives like this, scratching for lousy crumbs. We've got to get our fingers out.'

'Yeah,' said Tucker. 'You're right, Mish, you're right. For a start I'm going to talk to Alan's dad. Just to fill in, till I can get something better. Even credit accounts at Oxfam cost something.'

She smiled.

'And motorbikes cost more. And flash women like me! It's a good idea, Peter. As long as you don't forget you need a *real* job pretty soon.'

Tucker held her neck and kissed her, hard then softly. I'm not likely to, he thought. I've got plenty of incentives. But Alan's dad would be a start. And money would . . . The thoughts dissolved.

'I've got about a fiver left,' he whispered in her ear. 'Why don't we find somewhere warm. And very very dark . . .'

'Mmmmm,' went Mish.

Chapter Six

For all their hankering after something real to do, for all their aimlessness and boredom wandering the streets, the first job Mr Hargreaves set them on to was a swine. It started in jollity and banter, sure enough. But by the end of their first day, they had an inkling that working for a living was not quite the doddle – or the cure-all – they had always thought it would be. And of course, for Mr Hargreaves they were not working for a *living*. He had the perfect excuse for paying them peanuts – if he gave them more than a few quid they'd be breaking the benefit rules and they'd be sent to jail without collecting £200 for passing Go. In fact, though, he paid them even less than they could have declared. His other excuse was that *he* was struggling, too.

The morning started with a good laugh, mainly at Tommy Watson's expense. When Tucker had approached Alan the day after his great decision he'd been surprised, and relieved, to find that he had no persuading to do. 'Look,' he'd said. 'About working for your old man. You might think I'm a twat, but I'm desperate. I reckon – ' Alan had interrupted him. 'Don't grovel, Jenkins,' he'd said. 'So am I. I've already told him *I* would, and I said I'd try to rope you in. And Tommy.'

They'd not been able to find Tommy, although they'd combed the streets, done all the usual haunts, and even climbed four and a quarter million stairs to his flat because the lift was out of order. But they'd thought he'd be dead reluctant to commit himself to anything that smacked of labour. Not only was Tommy an idle git, but he was vain. He'd always sworn he'd never do a job that might make his hands dirty. Tommy was also slightly better off than them, because his mum bunged him more than they could ever wheedle.

But when they finally tracked him down, coming from a betting shop, he'd jumped at the offer like a shot. As they climbed into the back of Mr H's pick-up at eight o'clock next morning, they were still ragging him.

'Come on, Tom,' said Tucker. 'Admit it. When you've picked up your first wage packet, what you going to do with it? You almost took Alan's arm off when he offered you.'

Alan's father was climbing into the cab.

'The amount I'm paying, he's probably putting a down payment on a Roller,' he said. 'Or is it a helicopter you've got your eye on, Tom?'

Tommy kept his secret, as the ideas got wilder and wilder. But as they bounced past a fashion shop he gave the game away.

'D'you know,' he said, jerking a thumb at the lingerie displayed in the window. 'A pair of drawers in that place costs you eight pound fifty?'

He lived to regret it, naturally. They mocked him up hill and down dale. The general consensus was that carrying Allison's plastic bag around for a day or so that time had turned his brain. Eight pound fifty for a pair of knickers. Bloody Nora!

The laughter stopped when they arrived at the job. Mr Hargreaves opened up a lock-up shop while they piled onto the pavement. It was dingy, and dirty, and smelled. And it was full to the ceiling with junk, and rubbish, and broken furniture and fittings.

'Hey, Mr H!' said Tucker. 'I thought it was a paint job you was giving us. What is there to paint? You can't even see the bleeding walls!'

'Very funny, Tucker,' replied Alan's dad. 'Are you suggesting that they don't exist, just cause you can't see them? *First* off, you clean the crap out, right? *Then* you clean the paintwork down and give everything a good old scrub-off. *Then* you does the paint-job. Got it, my son?'

Tommy Watson was dismayed. Even his 'working' jeans were pretty snazzy. And as for what this lot would do to his hands!

'But it'll take us *ages*!' he said. 'It's filthy!'

Mr Hargreaves looked at them to see if they were pulling his leg.

'Are you a gang of lunatics or something?' he asked. 'Do you think working's easy? Or pleasant? Or a bundle of fun? Are you trying to wind me up?'

Alan recognised the symptoms. His dad was getting ratty. He flashed a look at his mates.

'We'll be all right, Dad,' he said. 'It's not what they expected, that's all. The only painting Tucker's ever done was the scenery for the school play. The teachers did the hard bits and he just sloshed the colours on. He still thinks he's a kid.'

'Well I'm not doing it without overalls,' said Tucker. 'You'll have to buy us the gear, Mr H. That's flat.'

'Yer,' Tommy agreed. Weakly.

'Right,' said Mr Hargreaves. 'In the bloody street, the lot of you. You can either start grafting, or you can piss off. Now. The choice is yours.'

His face had reddened. He wasn't kidding. The three boys looked at each other.

'You may not have noticed it,' went on Mr Hargreaves. 'You probably didn't even *recognise* it. But there's a skip outside this shop in the gutter, and it didn't *grow* there. It's there because I paid for it to be there. And the longer it stays there, the more it costs me. Now. Either get filling it, or sod off. Go away. And if you do, don't ever bloody think you'll work for me again. However short you are. Got it?'

Once they'd started, once Mr Hargreaves had driven off to whichever job *he* was grafting on, it wasn't quite so bad. They grumbled some more, but they got their jackets off and they got down to it. Most of the heavy stuff, the bust-up furniture, was in the middle of the shop, and after they'd shifted the bulkiest bits the job began to look at least doable. It was heavy work though, and filthy. After a couple of hours all three were covered in sweat and muck, with raw and aching hands. They called a halt and a rest when Tommy tore a finger on a nail sticking from a length of counter.

'God, look at that,' he said disgustedly. 'It's the first time I've ever seen blood washing dirt away.'

'It's the first time I've ever seen dirt on those pampered little hands,' said Tucker. 'I'm surprised someone as grand as you has even *got* blood. It ought to be blue, at least!'

'Hadn't you better take the rest of the week off to go to hospital?' said Al, with heavy irony. 'You might get lockjaw, you know!'

Tommy flicked a blob of blood from his finger end at Alan's face.

'It's you that needs lockjaw, Tubs,' he said. 'If you couldn't eat or drink for a month you might get down to ten stone or so. You might begin to pull some birds.'

Tucker laughed.

'He wouldn't know what to do with 'em if he did, would you Al? The only thing you and that McMahon used to do was row.'

Alan said nothing. Even the mention of Susi's name was painful.

Tommy asked him: 'How far did you get with Susi, Al? You know. How far up the scale?'

'Give over,' muttered Alan. 'We're not at Grange Hill now. We're not kids. Scale my arse.'

'Ooh God,' fantasised Tommy Watson. 'I'd like to scale Allison Powell. I'd like to climb all over her. She's a right little goer, she is.'

'Yeah,' said Tucker. 'It looks like it if even her drawers cost eight pound fifty! But she's not likely to drop 'em for a peasant like you, is she? Eight pound fifty's a week's money, mate!'

'Don't you be so sure,' said Tommy. 'I'm doing very nicely, thank you. How are you getting on with Mish?'

Tucker put on a very old man's voice.

'Can't grumble, Guv,' he said. 'The trouble is, she's insatiable. She's aged me she has, she's aged me. You'd never believe to look at me I'm only ninety six, now would you, Guv?'

'Seriously, though?' asked Tommy. 'How far have you got?'

'Never you bloody mind,' said Tucker. 'Shut up, anyway. You're making Alan drool.'

'Ah dry up,' said Alan grumpily. 'Let's get working, eh? You're both a pair of bullshit artists, that's what you are.'

Although he did not actually believe that, Alan was pretty nearly right. In the lunch hour, when Tucker and Tommy refused to go to the chippy with him because they had dates, he got dead depressed. It appeared to him that they were both in paradise, and he was in something that felt at times like hell. He returned to the shop alone, and sat alone amid the rubbish to eat his meat pie and chips. When he had finished them, he decided to take a walk. Try as he might, the direction he took was inevitable. It led to Susi's college. He hung about there, grubby, fat and miserable, for half an hour – like a sore thumb among the strolling students. He did not see her, though. But before he returned he went back to the chipshop and had another helping.

Far from having a warm and sexy time with Mish, however, Tucker spent his lunch break in a phone box. As for Tommy Watson, his little piece of paradise consisted of having his first row, and getting laughed at by a gang of schoolgirls. Both of which facts would probably have cheered Alan up no end, if he'd known about them. But there was not much chance of that, unfortunately.

Tucker was in a phone box because Michelle said he should be. She was there too, along with about fifty ten pence pieces and a copy of the local rag. Tucker, who'd had visions of a quiet beer and sandwich, with perhaps a little bodily contact thrown in, was fed up. But when he'd met her, she'd already brought the earliest possible edition of the paper, and gone through it, and ringed all the jobs that appeared even remotely possible.

'This is stupid, Mish,' he moaned. 'Everyone'll ring at dinnertime. And if they say to come along I couldn't anyway. I've *got* a job. I've got to be back there in an hour, or Alan's dad'll go ape.'

'*I* haven't though, have I? *I* could go. Don't be so selfish. And what do you mean, a job? He's just giving you a bit of pocket money, and working you like a slave for it, an'all. You're being exploited, Peter.'

Oh great, thought Tucker. Whose idea was it for him to get some ready cash?

'I know,' he said, trying to keep the peace. 'But you could ring any time. You could spend the afternoon doing it. I'm knackered, I need a rest.'

'You can rest when you get back to work,' said Michelle. 'Look, hold the paper. I'm trying this one first. For you. Read us out the number.'

The paper with the advert in had only been on the news stand for about an hour. But the line was engaged, solid. When they'd got the signal ten times in a row, they tried another one, this time for Michelle. Same story. It was twenty minutes before they rang a number and got through.

'Hello,' said Mish. 'I'm ringing about the job. I saw it in . . . oh. Oh. Yeah. Well thanks, anyway.'

She put the phone down and made a face.

'Gone,' she said. 'Bloody hell, Tucker.'

'Yeah,' he said. 'Perhaps we'd better have a drink after all.'

Hopefully.

'Piss off,' she said. 'What's the next one ringed?'

Outside Brookdale School, Tommy Watson was having an equally frustrating time. He'd been walking up and down the pavement for ages with Allison, and they were getting nowhere. She was – it seemed to him – distant, unfriendly, coy, and playing hard to get. He couldn't understand it.

'But Alli,' he said. 'We've been out lots of times now. *Why* won't you say you won't see him again?'

'I've *told* you,' replied Allison. 'I'm not going to be trapped into anything. I'm fifteen years old, Tommy. I'm going to see *whoever* I like, *whenever* I like.'

'But *Passmore*,' said Tommy, in anguish. 'He's a thug, Allison. He's a bloody nutcase, a skin.'

'He's not that bad,' said Allison. 'It's show, a lot of it. He's always been very good to me.'

'Hah,' responded Tommy. 'He's about as good as a three-inch LP.'

Allison gave him a withering look. Her lively face was

52

serious, she was trying to get something over to him.

'Very amusing I'm sure,' she said. 'Look, Tommy, you don't own me, right? I'm not a piece of property. I'm a girl. A person.'

Where have I heard that before, she thought. I was telling Ralph it not so long ago. *Why* do these boys want to take *control*? Who do they think they *are*? Why couldn't they just go out with you, and enjoy themselves, and have a laugh? She did not *want* to be a possession. Anybody's possession.

'So you're going to go out with Passmore again, are you?' asked Tommy, bitterly.

She almost screamed.

'No! For God's sake *no*. I never said that. I have no intention of ever *seeing* him again, right? But I wouldn't run a mile if I did. I'd *talk* to him, I'd have a *coffee*. But I am *not* going to go out with him again.'

Tommy shook his head.

'So what *are* you saying then? Just what the *hell* are you saying?'

Allison stopped. Tommy stopped also. They stood there on the pavement, with Allison's schoolmates milling past, many of them smirking knowingly.

'I'm not saying anything,' she said. 'I'm trying to keep my temper. I like you, I like you a lot. I like going out with you and I'm not going to stop – unless you drive me crazy with all this stuff. But you do *not* own me. Now. I'm going back to school.'

She moved off so suddenly that Tommy was left gaping. He began to follow, but she was running. To have done that, with all her pals about, would have made him look ridiculous. He put on a bold, uncaring face and glanced at his watch. Smashing, he thought. Our very first row. And we haven't even had a real good grope yet. Smashing.

That night, after their first day's work, the boys felt like a drink. They were exhausted, and dirty, and depressed. After a pint they set off on the trudge for home, and they passed along the edge of the flats where Michelle lived. Tucker was due to meet her later, and he half hoped he might bump into her, and make some excuse. All he really fancied was to prop himself up in an armchair and watch the box. Trouble was, he didn't know the number of her flat, although he knew the block.

But as they turned the corner into a courtyard, Tucker, Alan and Tommy came face to face with Michelle. She was standing by a doorway, and she was with Allison. Turning away from them and disappearing into the door, was a youth. Big boots, braces, and a pork-pie hat. It could only be one guy in the world. Passmore.

As they stood there, open-mouthed and goggle-eyed, the door slammed shut behind him. Allison and Michelle gaped back.

Tommy and Michelle spoke simultaneously.

'Tucker,' said Michelle.

'Allison,' said Tommy Watson.

Alan Hargreaves found it difficult to suppress a little smile.

Chapter Seven

Maybe because they knew that Passmore was behind the front door, the three boys did not move towards it. They waited for the girls to collect their wits together and come to them. They did not have long to wait.

Michelle was the first to speak. She spoke to Tucker.

'Hi,' she said. 'Fancy meeting you here. Looking for someone, were you?'

It was not Tucker who spoke next, however. Tommy, trying to hide the fact that he was completely upset, said to Allison: 'That was quick, then. After what you said at dinnertime.'

Allison coloured.

'*I* remember what I said at lunchtime, Tommy. Even if you don't. I said I'd meet who I wanted, when I wanted, where I wanted.'

Alan looked from one to another of them. His faint feeling of elation had gone. Gawd, what a cock-up. Why didn't anything ever go right?

'Correct,' said Tommy. 'I can't fault you on that, Miss Powell. Well, thanks, anyway.'

He turned, as if he was going to stalk off. Allison grabbed his sleeve.

'Look, you fool,' she said. 'Hadn't you better ask me what I'm doing here? I'm trying to keep my cool, Tommy, but you're not helping much. It's a bit insulting, you know. I don't like people who jump to conclusions. Especially dirty ones.'

'What were *you* doing with Passmore, anyway?' got in Tucker to Michelle. 'I –'

'Shut up and listen,' said Michelle. 'Go on, Alli. You tell him.'

'I didn't even know you two knew each other,' said Tommy, sulkily. 'Come on then. Why *are* you here? What were you talking to that . . . bloke about?'

'I came to get some albums back,' said Allison. She made a gesture with a bag she was carrying. 'I lent him some when we were . . . going around together. All right?'

'Oh.' Tommy felt a fool, and looked it. 'Oh, I – '

'Yeah,' said Allison. 'You thought. Or didn't think, more like. It wasn't exactly a friendly meeting, I can tell you. And if you don't believe me, ask Mish.'

'That's right,' said Mish. 'Daggers drawn they were. Ralph didn't seem that pleased to see you at all, did he Alli?'

The two girls giggled. Tucker found it rather irritating.

'I don't think it's very funny,' he said. 'What's the big joke? And if Allison was getting records, what's your excuse?'

'Oh, listen to Lord Jenkins! What's my excuse indeed!' She wagged a finger provocatively under his nose. 'I don't need excuses,' she said. 'And don't you forget it, right? Excuses!'

She and Allison went off into another ripple of giggles. Tucker was seeing red.

'What's Passmore to you, anyway?' he demanded. 'Why didn't you tell me you knew him?'

'What are you talking about? I didn't know *you* knew him till I mentioned your name just now. But now he knows about us he's in a real good humour, I don't think. What with that and Alli messing around with Tom. It's a good job he didn't spot you here. It would have been an Old Bill job.'

'And I suppose you'd have been on *his* side?' said Tucker. 'Look, just what is that berk to you?'

'Well,' said Michelle. 'Let's say I'm very fond of him. Let's say I love him, even. How will that do?'

Tucker could not believe his ears. He felt as if someone had removed his stomach. And Michelle was smiling! He almost stuttered.

'What do you . . . what do you mean?' Then he shook his head, hard. 'Come on, Alan. Come on, Tom. Let's go, I'm sick of this.'

Allison smiled at Tucker, a big, open smile. Despite himself, he almost responded. Somehow it helped, it dulled the pain. But his jealousy and anger soured it.

Allison said: 'Oh come on, Mish. Don't be too rotten. Can't you see he's suffering?'

'Huh,' went Michelle. 'He bloody deserves to, too. Stupid, possessive . . .'

'Oh come on, Mish, come on.'

Allison's pretty eyes shone on Tucker with real sympathy. He found himself looking into hers.

'What's she on about?' he asked. 'What's going on? For crying out loud, what's going on?'

'He's my bloody *brother*, you stupid berk,' said Michelle. 'Ralph Passmore is my brother. Now do you get it, you dozy sod?'

'But your name's not . . . you're not called . . . *Bloody Nora!*'

'Yes,' said Michelle patiently. 'But he's still my brother, isn't he? It's the twentieth century, Peter. People get divorced. Marriages break up. But whichever way you cut it, he's my brother. That pork-pie hatted freak's our kid. Got it?'

Alan spoke for the first time.

'You poor sod, Mish,' he said. 'You have my deepest sympathy.'

Later on that night, exhaustion forgotten, the two couples went out as a foursome. They invited Alan, but he picked up the tone of voice at three hundred yards, and told them he was knackered. He was, but that was not the point. Luckily, his old man was still as pleased as Punch about him working at long last, so he bought some tins of ale and they watched the telly happily enough till Alan crashed out, pretty early.

The others also bought some cans, and went to Tommy's flat. Tommy's Mum was always out at nights, and he could hardly remember when he'd last seen his old feller, so when they'd kicked his kid sister Debbie into the kitchen to do her French homework, they colonised the living room to do some French kissing.

Somehow or other, though, they couldn't concentrate. They kept breaking off as pairs of lovers to talk as four friends. Ralph Passmore was the subject, every time.

'Fancy me not knowing you and Mish was friends,' said Tommy. 'I've never seen you round together, like.'

'There is a reason,' laughed Michelle.

'No!' said Allison. 'Mish don't! You'll embarrass me!'

'Don't be so daft,' replied Michelle. 'I don't mind. I'm beginning to agree with you, anyway.'

Tucker put his beer down.

'Ladies, I know it must be jolly fun to have a secret, but it could get tedious. "Reasons", "embarrassment"? Out with it, sir! What are you beginning to agree with?'

'Oh it's just a friend of mine, that's all. Alli can't stand the sight of her. So all the time I knock around with her, Alli stays away.'

'Silly really,' said Allison. 'But she is a . . .'

'She can be difficult,' finished Mish. 'You met her, Tucker. Down at the Dole House. You didn't reckon much to her neither.'

'Bloody hell! Not that snooty piece with the long brown hair who said she was pregnant!'

'What!' went Allison. 'Mandy pregnant! Oh *Mish*!'

'No no no! Tucker you are a fool! No look, leave it at this: she is a bit of a pain sometimes. For instance – since I took up with you, I haven't hardly seen her. She don't approve, right? She thinks you're an immature, stupid, witless – '

Tommy put in: 'You said there was something wrong with her! She sounds like a perfect judge of character to me!'

'*Is* she pregnant, though?' asked Allison. 'She's only sixteen.'

'No,' said Mish. 'But she thought she was, a couple of months ago. Tucker's only scandal-spreading, take no notice.'

Next time the conversation got going, Tucker asked Michelle: 'You know you said you was fond of Passmore, like? You said you sort of loved him? Is that right? You can't do really, can you?'

Allison almost dropped herself in it by saying what she'd felt about him, but stopped in time. She got a hard look from Tommy, though, and blushed faintly. She covered that up by kissing him passionately. Well, that's what she made it feel like.

Michelle considered.

'I dunno really,' she said. 'I mean, you can't be indifferent, can you? You always feel something for your family, don't you? And he can be a real good laugh, honest. I do worry about him, though.'

'Why?' joked Tommy. 'Because he's a raving psychopath?'

Michelle did not smile. It was quite a time before she answered.

'Sometimes he can be great,' she said. 'When he's on his own he can be nice, and kind, and . . . stuff. But sometimes . . . well, I expect Alli could tell . . . Well, yeah. Sometimes he frightens me.'

Allison had tensed in Tommy's arms, sitting on the sofa. She knew exactly what Michelle meant, but she wasn't going to say anything, obviously. In a way, she was only with Tommy because . . . her mind shied away from the thought. Even meeting Ralph today had confused her. After that last, awful row, she'd supposed she'd merely hate him. But when he'd opened the door. If Michelle had not been there too . . .

She became aware that Tommy was staring at her, willing her to make a statement. Michelle noticed it also, and came to her rescue. She said seriously: 'I'll tell you one thing, though. He's got it in for you two now. When it came out today that me and Tucker were going out. On top of what he suspects about Tommy and Allison. Jesus.'

'Suspects?' said Tommy. 'Does he actually know?'

Both girls shrugged.

'He's got his friends. He's got spies. Anyway, he doesn't bother much with facts, doesn't brother dear. It's enough that he suspects. You and his best girl.'

'Well bloody hell,' said Tommy, faintly. 'Alli's a free agent, though. What's it got to do with him?'

'What's it got to do with him who *I* go out with?' retorted Michelle. 'I'm his sister, not his pet rabbit. But he seems to think he's got the right to stick his oar in. I'm just warning you, that's all.'

There was a silence. They thought their thoughts.

'He's got a tattoo on his arm,' said Allison. She looked vaguely frightened at the memory. 'It says Allison. It says my name.'

Tucker joked: 'Spelt wrong, I suppose!'

'No,' said Allison. 'Spelt right. Two ells. He told me he had it done to show how serious he was.'

Tucker looked at Allison's face. Concerned; almost afraid. A thought swept into his mind so fast it shocked him. He wanted to look after her, to cuddle her. Christ, he thought. Allison Powell. I don't half fancy you. Oh baby; don't I just!

It was four days later before Ralph Passmore made a move, and it was such a violent one that the boys could scarcely believe he'd done it. It proved one thing anyway – Michelle had not been exaggerating.

It came about through their own stupidity, in part, which made it worse. What's more, it got them into lumber with Alan's dad.

The morning started fine. They were round at the shop, and they'd had a good night out the night before, and Tucker was exultant anyway. He was pretty certain – although not a hundred per cent – that his Mum was going to cough the motorbike cash. Which, apart from anything else, had helped to keep his mind off Allison, and his growing feeling that something had to happen with her, soon.

Mr H had dropped them off and gone away, which had caused the usual banter among the boys. Alan was used to his father's disappearing acts, because he knew that the only way a jobbing builder could survive was to be doing at least three things at once. But the other two were unconvinced. They reckoned Mr H must have at least one woman waiting for him every morning, if not two or three.

'Why don't you admit it, Al?' said Tommy Watson. 'He's a dirty old ram. He's gone off humping housewives, not bags of plaster.'

'If only you knew,' Alan replied. 'Nobody loves a builder. It's not like a milkman, that turns up every day. In this business you've got to swear black and white to at least a dozen women you'll have their job done by Tuesday at the latest, and you know damn well you can't be there for a fortnight. It makes you bleeding popular, I can tell you.'

'Nah,' said Tucker. 'He's got that glint in his eye, your old father. He must have been quite a good-looker once, as well, before he grew that beer gut. Tommy'll be like him when he's ninety nine.'

They carried on the backchat while they cleared out the last of the rubbish to the skip. This was lightweight stuff, stripped paper and so on. They were so well into the job now that everything was ready for the off. The walls were cleaned, the undercoat was ready, the brushes had been prepared. On one of their trips outside they spotted Passmore on the other side of the street, and they were so elated that they jeered at him, in an almost matey way. Passmore, alone, walked on.

By eleven o'clock, still acting like a group of school kids on an outing to the beach, they were ready to start painting. It was Alan who made the big decision.

'Look, lads,' he said, as Tucker prised the lid off the first five-litre can of undercoat. 'This calls for a celebration. By strange coincidence we're about to start on the stroke of opening time. So how about it?'

What a great idea! The nearest pub was a two-minute walk away, and they were all quite flush, for them.

'Just a quick half,' said Alan. 'You know my old man. He *might* pop back, and he'd go bananas if he thought we was slacking. We'll only be two ticks. Agreed?'

Agreed. Tucker jammed the lid back on, loosely. Tommy picked up his bomber-jacket, and they hustled out.

They were only going for two ticks. Alan, who'd been left in charge, of course, didn't even bother to lock the door . . .

Chapter Eight

Ralph Passmore, although he had Brains with him now, didn't intend to start a fight or anything like that. But he did just think they'd pop their heads into the shop and issue some warnings. Or threats, even. As he explained to the living skull beside him, he was going to have them soon, but he wanted them to sweat first.

'I dunno why you're bothering, Chief,' said Brains as they swaggered down the street frightening old ladies with their shoulders and their boots. 'No slag's worth it, surely? I mean, there's plenty of other tarts about, in'there?'

'Oh yeah,' said Passmore. 'She's nothing to me. Just a bit of fun to go round with some high-class crumpet for a change. Nah, it's the principle of the thing, ain't it?'

'If you say so, Boss. I don't give a shit for principles myself, like. But I do like a bundle. You just give me the nod when you're ready, right?'

They approached the window of the shop, and slowed. Passmore looked through, then swore with disappointment. He moved into the doorway, pressing his face against the glass for a clearer view.

'The twats ain't here,' he said. 'Bloody hell.'

He automatically tried the handle.

'*Bloody* hell! It's open!'

Down the pub, inevitably, one quick half had led to another. After twenty minutes, there was a serious debate about going back.

'Oh come on, Al,' said Tucker. 'It's a celebration, remember. Your dad won't pop in till dinnertime. He'll be cuddling up to some frustrated housewife somewhere.'

'That's not the point,' said Alan. 'I've left the shop unlocked. Anyone could go in.'

'Nobody ever has, though, have they? Come on, have another drink, you fat freak.'

Tommy finished off his glass.

'I'm going back anyway,' he said. 'I'm on a promise, dinnertime. I don't want to be dying for a pee all the time, do I? You two have another one, all right?'

That clinched that. It was better than working for a living, after all.

Brains and Passmore just couldn't believe their luck. They were grinning like a pair of circus clowns.

'Well how nice,' said Passmore. 'How nice of them to remember us like that. How nice to leave a job for two of the unfortunate unemployed.'

He reached for a screwdriver and began to prise the lid off a paint pot. Brains discovered Tucker's, already practically undone.

'I always wanted to be a decorator,' he said. 'My hero was a housepainter. Old Adolf Hitler. White paint, too. He'd have approved of that!'

Ralph, impatient with prising, jabbed at the lid with the screwdriver until he punctured it. The pair of them were ready simultaneously. They stood solemnly side by side.

'I now declare this paint shop open,' said Passmore. 'On the count of three, Mister Mate.'

'Aye aye, cap'n!'

'Ready. Aim. Fire!'

Two five-litre gushes of white undercoat shot across the shop and hit the walls. It was magnificent. Brains and Passmore laughed delightedly.

'Now that's artistic,' said Brains. 'You've got a gift, you have, Chief. A definite gift.'

They attacked the stack of paint pots with gusto. Both of them used screwdrivers, jabbing and stabbing until the lids pulled off, then hurling them at all the walls in turn. Passmore, to the amazement of passers-by, chucked the contents of a can at the plate-glass window. A motorist nearly drove up a lamp standard.

Tommy Watson, ambling back along the road, saw the sudden white stain flash across the window. Too amazed to think caution, he raced to the doorway and burst through. Before he could burst out again, he was cornered.

'*Bloody* Nora! Have you gone bloody *mad*!'

Brains grabbed Tommy's shoulder and shoved him up against a wall. He gave him a playful crack across the face that nearly broke his neck, then prepared to punch him properly.

'Back off!' yelled Passmore. 'Stand clear. I'm going to do a whitewash job!'

Brains sprang to one side and Tommy, seeing what was coming, tried to duck and cover his face.

But it was too late. Half a can of paint hit him full in the face and chest, with solid force. He'd managed to get his eyes closed, but it got up his nose and into his mouth. He fell forward to his knees, spitting, blind and horrified.

If he hadn't looked in such a bad way, Brains and Passmore would probably have given him a kicking. But his choking coughs unnerved them. If he was going to die, they didn't want to be there.

'Come on,' said Brains. 'Party's over.'

'You bastard,' choked Tommy, on the floor. 'You lousy bastard, Passmore.'

'Oh piss off, you,' snarled Passmore. 'You'll get a lot worse than this, you will. And don't say you didn't get a warning, will you? And pass it on to that twat that's messing with my sister. I *do not like* it.'

Tommy heard the door slam. He cleared the paint from around his eyes and tried to open one. It hurt.

A celebration drink, he thought. But he didn't feel like laughing . . .

When Alan's father arrived in the pick-up half an hour later he only saved himself from having his first heart attack by going into a fury as cold and bleak as ice. He stared at the scene of devastation for a full minute before he spoke. The boys stopped cleaning Tommy up and reverted to their childhoods. They stood as still as primary kids getting a wigging from the head. They did not move, they did not even shuffle, while Mr Hargreaves took it in. At last he spoke. He spoke to his son.

'You useless, idle, fat, stupid, selfish little *bastard*,' he said. 'I suppose this is your way of showing me your loyalty.'

Tucker and Tommy Watson dropped their eyes to the floor. To the pools of white undercoat they were standing in.

'Dad,' said Alan. His voice was choked. 'It wasn't – '

'Shut up, you useless *prat*,' his father snapped. 'I don't want to even *hear* it.'

Tommy, bright red under his covering of diluted paint and turpentine, said: 'Honest, Mr. H. It wasn't us. We weren't larking. Some skins – '

'How many skins?' said Mr Hargreaves. 'An army? What did you do? Invite them in? And why are you the only one in warpaint, eh? You make me tired. You make me sick. The lot of you.'

He turned back to Alan. Alan was upset by his father's venom and unfairness. He was trembling.

'I left you in charge,' his father said. 'And this is what I get. I don't want to hear the story, I'm not interested. I wouldn't believe you anyway, you're not someone I can trust.'

Alan's chest began to shake. He could hardly stop a sob from breaking out. He dared not even try to open his mouth in self-defence.

'Get it cleared up,' said Mr Hargreaves. 'All of you. If you catch it before it dries you'll get the worst off. The paint comes from your wages. And the hire of the sander to get the floorboards clean. And the turps and thinners. And the detergent and the scrubbing brushes. Everything.'

'I'll have to go and change,' said Tommy. His voice was squeaky. 'I'll have to get cleaned up.'

Mr Hargreaves looked at him contemptuously.

'Tommy,' he said. 'You can do what you bloody well like. I don't give a toss. But the longer you're away the less time you'll be putting in to pay your debts off. And the more work your mates will have to do. Understand?'

'Yes,' said Tommy. Five minutes ago he'd felt hard done by. Now he felt ashamed. Mr Hargreaves turned to the door.

'I'm going,' he said. 'I don't trust myself to stay. I don't trust myself to talk to you.'

No one spoke until the pick-up had pulled away and gone.

It was ten minutes before Alan emerged from the back room. Tommy had gone off home, feeling an absolute superwally, to change as quickly as possible. Tucker had started to clean up, then given up. It looked impossible. It didn't seem likely that the shop would ever look reasonable again.

Alan came out of the back quietly, and found his mate sitting on a box.

'You all right?' he said.

'Yeah. You?'

'Yeah,' said Alan. 'What a bastard, eh?'

'Who? Passmore or your dad?'

'I meant Passmore, matter of fact,' he said. 'For once in my life I suppose I think my old man's justified. We bolloxed it, Tucker. We really bolloxed it.'

'Yeah.'

Alan slumped down onto the floor. The fact that he was sitting in a pool of paint did not bother him. Why should it?

'But what are we going to do?' he said.

'Kill the bastard,' said Tucker. 'I'd like to string him up. I'd like to boil him in oil, with his bastard mate. I'd like to cut his balls off with a blunt knife. A plastic knife. I'd like to stick an air hose up his arse and blow his eyeballs out.'

'I think I'll call the cops,' said Alan. 'I think we ought to set the law on him.'

Tucker glanced at Alan, shaken.

'You must be joking, mate,' he said. 'You must be off your rocker. None of that, Al. Leave it out, son.'

'Why? Why not call the police? They've committed criminal damage, Tucker. They've gone ten feet over this time. We could get the buggers right in lumber.'

Tucker Jenkins got to his feet. He walked across and waved his hand in front of Alan's face. Negative.

'No, Alan,' he said. 'You're raving, pal. We couldn't prove a thing. The cops would laugh at us. And then they'd talk to the Dole. *No.*'

'We're not breaking any laws,' said Alan. 'We could –'

'Oh shuddup,' said Tucker. 'It's out, mate. No fuzz. Impossible. Apart from anything else, what do you think that bloody Passmore would do if we did? Are you cracked? He'd kill us, son. Stone bleeding dead. He'd kill us.'

'So what do we do then? Let him get away with it? Send him a thank you letter? You said you'd cut his balls off, Tucker, but you won't. You'll let him off the bloody hook.'

'I?' said Tucker. 'Alan, we're all of us in this, I can't take him on my own. Far bloody from it. The question is, can we take him all together?'

They jumped a foot in the air as the door opened, but it was only Tommy. He looked so funny that they laughed. He was pink and scrubbed, with his damp curls hanging down beside his ears. But his hair was streaked and stringy with paint, and there were traces of it on all the skin exposed.

He was quite put out by their attitude.

'Bloody hell,' he said. 'It's not a laughing matter, this. I could have drowned, you know.'

'What?' said Tucker. 'In the bath? You need more practice, mate!'

Chapter Nine

Urgent as the need to get revenge was, there were other things in life more urgent. Number One was cleaning up the worst of the paint before it dried – and it was drying pretty rapidly. They boiled water in the back, they got pints and pints of turps substitute from down the road, they got scrubbing and scraping as if there was no tomorrow. They worked harder than they'd ever worked before, and they never forgot this fact: not only were they not getting paid for doing it, but all the paint they scraped up and wiped away was down to them to buy. It was a total loss and it was a double loss. But they kept at it till they were almost too knackered to stand.

Number Two on the urgency stakes for Tucker, was to carry on the conversation he'd been having with his mum over the money for the motorbike. As soon as they agreed to call it a day, he was raring to go home. He wouldn't go with Tommy and Alan for a pint, he said, he had some secret business.

'Oh yeah,' said Tommy. 'Some secret! It wouldn't be to do with a girl called Michelle would it? A girl with a psycho for a brother?'

'No,' said Tucker. 'It would not. It would be to do with something a sight more important than that.'

'Oh!' said Tom. 'I'll tell Michelle you said that!'

Alan looked around the shop. It still looked terrible, although the improvement was fantastic.

'Early start tomorrow, men,' he said. 'We've broke the back of it. We've got the worst off. See you at the yard at –'

'Dole House day,' said Tom. 'Why d'you think we've worked our knicks off this afternoon? We've got to sign on in the morning.'

'Oh,' said Al. 'That'll please my father; I'd forgot. Look, Tom, are you coming for a drink? I need some

Dutch courage before I face him, know what I mean? If I had the loot I'd get rat-legged.'

'We..ell,' went Tommy. 'I'm meant to be seeing Alli soon. We're dead late, you know.'

Tucker laughed.

'Do yourself a favour, mate,' he said. 'Stay away. She'll not thank you for turning up looking like the Dulux dog. Go and have a pint.'

Tommy hardly wavered.

'Yeah,' he said. 'Bugger it, I will. She'll never know if I stand her up. I'll tell her I was taken ill. I do look pale, you must admit!'

They left the shop. Tucker felt secretly pleased. So Tommy would stand her up, would he? Good. He liked that. He liked that very much.

On the way home, Tucker did something extremely obvious. He stopped at a florists that was open late, and he bought his Mum some flowers. He didn't know what they were called or anything sophisticated, he bought them by price. The second cheapest bunch they had. Not the cheapest, naturally. He wasn't a cheapskate, after all!

It was obvious, but it worked. His mother positively glowed.

'Oh Peter,' she said. 'How nice of you! Aren't they lovely!'

She knew it meant he wanted something, and she knew exactly what it was, but that didn't appear to matter. She found a vase, and popped them in, and filled it up with water from the kitchen tap.

'Do you want a bath before your tea, dear?' she asked. 'You're all covered in white paint. Have you had a successful day?'

Tucker set off for the bathroom.

'I'll have a wash,' he said. 'I'm too weary to get in the bath, I'd only go to kip. Yeah, not bad, thanks. We're getting on a treat. Is Dad in?'

'Been and gone,' she said. 'He's doing darts tonight or something. That's his story, anyway.'

You crafty swine, thought Tucker as he scrubbed away at the undercoat. Flowers, keeping your mouth shut about the cock-up with the job, and Dad safely out with his mates. She'll be like putty in your hands.

He was so polite and chatty at tea-time, he praised and thanked her so fulsomely for the wonderful meal, that his Mum could hardly stop from giggling. While he was wolfing down his pudding she dropped in casually: 'Is there something on your mind, love? Something you want to ask? You seem very eager to please, all of a sudden.'

She'd caught him with his mouth full, so he could only nod indignantly and blush.

'No ulterior motive?' she laughed. 'It wouldn't be anything to do with borrowing a hundred pounds for a motorbike?'

By the time he'd cleared his mouth sufficiently to answer, he'd decided to come clean. Why mess about with his Mum? She either would or she wouldn't. And since he'd mended his ways . . .

'Well I *have* done my best to change, Mum, you must admit,' he said. 'I've got a job and I'm working like an absolute lunatic. It's slave labour, we're being totally exploited. But I'm keeping at it, I haven't missed a minute.'

'I know you haven't, love,' she said. 'And I'm very proud of you, Peter.'

'*And* I've paid you back three pound fifty of what I owe you,' he went on. 'And there'll be more to come, Mum, I promise you.'

'Three pounds forty four,' she said, smiling. 'Yes, Peter, it's smashing. I was beginning to wonder if you had it in you. It looks as if you have.'

Tucker swallowed another mouthful, hastily.

'This thing for Alan's Dad's not the end of it, either,' he said. 'I haven't given up looking for a proper job. Full time and a living wage. Having a bike would help, you know. I could zip down for interviews before the others. I could take on offers miles away, not just round here.'

She was nodding at every hurried sentence. She was taking the Mick something rotten. Tucker got excited. He was sure she'd made her mind up. He was sure he'd won.

70

'Well?'

'Look, Peter, love,' she said. Her smile faded, and Tucker's dropped off his face so hard he almost heard it hit the table. She shook her head.

'No, no!' she said. 'Don't look like that. The answer's yes. It's just that – '

She didn't get the chance to finish. Tucker was out of his seat and dancing round the room. He was roaring with delight. He knocked the remains of his pudding off the table and caught the dish so deftly he didn't spill a morsel.

'Oh Mum!' he yelled. 'You're wonderful. Come here for a kiss! I'll do the washing up!'

'There are *conditions,* Peter. It's not just a case of picking up a hundred pounds. There are *conditions.*'

'Anything, oh Wonderwoman Ma of mine,' he said. 'I'll do the washing up *tomorrow,* as well.'

'Good God,' she laughed. 'Nothing as difficult as *that,* love. I'm not a heartless woman!'

'You're great,' he said. 'You're bloody gorgeous, Mum. When can I have the money?'

The conditions weren't all that onerous, when he finally got to hear them, and as Tucker turned them over in his mind next morning, trudging along to Merve the Swerve's, he figured he could just about afford to live. Just about.

They were to do with money, naturally. Because although Tucker had turned over a new leaf for a week or so, his mother didn't trust him very far – about as far, in fact, as she could chuck him. They'd sat down and done their sums together, and what with his benefit, and the bit he got from Mr Hargreaves, it could just about be made to balance out. The trouble was, that the 'out' side was so much bigger than the 'in'. There was road tax, insurance, fuel, food, drink, fun, rent – and paying back his Mum. It was horrendous, written down on paper. It made him thirsty just to think about the incredible amount of beer he wouldn't be able to afford! And as for what Michelle would say! A trip to the movies would be like a trip to the moon now. Impossible.

But as Tucker approached the grotty garage inhabited by the demon biker, his heart began to lift. He felt like Toad of Toad Hall when he saw a motor car to nick. He could smell the open road!

He'd left it till long after ten to call on Merve, because he figured he was not the type to get up at the crack of dawn. In fact, he half expected to find the garage locked up and deserted. But he heard the ring of steel on steel. He heard the thumping of a bass line on the trannie. He heard Merve swearing, short and sharp, when he dropped something with a clatter.

'Hello, Merve,' said Tucker. 'Mind you don't drop that bracket!'

As Merve greeted him, Tucker took in the contents of the garage, and his racing heart slowed down a beat or two. She was there! The little sweetheart was waiting for him! Merve hadn't flogged her to another!

'Hiya, Jenk. You're a big surprise. I said a day or two, didn't I? I thought you'd bludged.'

'Nah,' said Tucker. 'Busy, wasn't I? Well – why bullshit, Merve? I couldn't raise the cash.'

Mervyn's oil-smeared face fell slightly.

'Oh, sorry to hear that,' he said. 'I thought I had a sale. What do you want, then? I can't hang on for ever. How much did I say? Eighty? How about sixty five? Can you run to that?'

Tucker almost gasped. Jesus Christ, I'm hearing things, he thought. Keep cool, Jenkins. Don't let him see you're rattled. Think fast.

Jenkins thought fast. He was famous for it.

'Bloody hell, Merve,' he said grouchily. 'It must be knackered if you're that desperate.'

Merve the Swerve gave a good-natured chuckle.

'You cheeky fart. That's my last offer, Jenk. Either say yes, or piss off. Pronto. I'm busy.'

'Too busy to give me a demo?'

'If you've got the money, no. If you haven't, yes.'

'Close your eyes then while I get it out of me stocking top,' said Tucker. 'I don't want to overheat your blood.'

He pulled his wallet out and flashed the contents. Time

72

later to extract the unexpected bonus of fifteen buckshee smackers. Merve nodded briefly.

'Get your helmet on,' he said. 'I trust you're wearing your brown underpants? This bike may be vintage, kid, but it goes like a bat. You'll probably wish you'd left your cash at home by the time I've finished with you.'

'Try me,' said Tucker. A little apprehensively. Mervyn smiled at him, a biker's smile.

'You asked for it,' he said.

The ride started slowly, for Merve was large, the engine was cold, and the bike was hardly in the big league, powerwise. But it cornered well, and braked all right, and seemed to run sweetly enough. But when they got onto a stretch of crowded dual carriageway, Mervyn began to put it through its paces. Tucker tightened his arms round the big, muscly waist in front of him and smelled Merve's sweat. Pretty soon, he could smell his own.

Merve the Swerve had lived with bikes for years. He did things with this one that made Tucker close his eyes. He whipped the gearbox unmercifully, keeping the engine revs close to the top of their range most of the time to squeeze the utmost power out of the small cylinder. He wove in and out of traffic, bounced over verges to gain a hundred yards, and made the footrests spark as he screamed round corners at what felt like suicidal speeds. At roundabouts he overtook almost everything, drifting from lane to lane to get the best advantage. The odd car driver, annoyed at being burned off, tried to kill them in the time-honoured manner, but Mervyn evaded every gambit with amused contempt. Every time Tucker saw his face, he was smiling. He was happy. He was relaxed.

He was brilliant, there was no denying it. It was not long before Tucker's fear had gone. He became relaxed, his body moved as one with Mervyn's. A smile of his own grew on his face. He thought of Mr Toad again, a happy thought. The open road. Fantastic.

Back at the garage, Merve pulled the bike onto its stand and plonked his helmet on a bench.

'There you are, Jenk,' he said. 'I told you it was sweet, didn't I? I bet you thought I was trying to palm you off with crap. I wouldn't, kid. I love bikes. You just learn to drive it properly, right? Don't kill yourself. It's far too easy, that.'

While Tucker peeled off sixty five from his roll, Mervyn even dug out a pair of tattered L-plates and put them on the bike with elastic bands.

'It's taxed for a month yet,' he said. 'But you'll need insurance. There's the details, there's the number of my broker. Telephone's in the corner over there. Ring 'em up and tell him what you want. Immediate cover, you pay in a week or so. All right, champion?'

Tucker nodded, almost speechless.

'Thanks, Merve,' he said. 'Thanks a million. You've been great. Honestly.'

Merve the Swerve smiled.

'Welcome to the gang, Jenk. Welcome to the gang. Just don't kill yourself.'

Tucker set off for the Dole House in a different manner altogether. Where Merve had driven brilliantly but furiously, he proceeded with extreme caution at slow speed. He'd driven bikes before, he knew his way around the gearbox and the clutch and so on. But he wasn't making any mistakes, and he wasn't playing any games. He felt almost impossibly happy, it had so far been the perfect day.

Up in front of him, walking along the pavement by the park, he saw a girl in uniform that he knew. He glanced over his shoulder, indicated, eased back the throttle, and drew up beside her.

'Hi, Allison!'

Allison Powell turned, looked puzzled, then recognised him.

'Tucker! What you doing on that thing, then?'

'It's mine,' he said. 'I've just bought it off a mate. What d'you reckon?'

Allison seemed more interested in looking *him* up and down. She giggled.

74

'I don't know anything about motorbikes,' she said. 'But you look dead sexy in that helmet.'

She put her hand up to her mouth and went red. Tucker's mouth went suddenly dry.

'Allison,' he croaked. 'I . . . I mean . . .'

Allison's face became scarlet.

'I've got to go,' she said. 'I've had two lessons off for the dentist, and I've got to meet my Mum. Have you seen Tommy? He was meant to meet me yesterday. I hope he isn't ill.'

'He's not,' said Tucker. It just popped out. Oh shit. All's fair in love and war. 'He was . . . it was . . . Look – I'll give you a lift. Come for a ride.'

'No!' said Allison. 'My dad would kill me! But . . . but . . .'

'I've got a crash-hat for you,' said Tucker, indicating the spare strapped to the carrier. 'I'll take me plates off. We'll be all right.'

Allison's lovely eyes widened.

'But Tucker. You could lose your licence. You're crazy.'

It's now or never, Jenkins. He gulped.

'I think I am,' he said. 'I think I'm in love, Allison.'

He licked his lips.

'With you.'

Chapter Ten

Meeting Tommy at the benefit just a little later was a pretty weird experience for Tucker. He knew he'd be there, and he'd have done anything to avoid it, but he had to go, natch. More money didn't grow on trees *now*, than ever before! He had a hungry bike to feed.

His driving, after Allison had scuttled off, had deteriorated quite badly. In fact, he'd almost gone under the back of a juggernaut at a roundabout, and it would not have been the driver's fault. When he arrived at the big airy building with its millions of scurrying unemployed, his attitude to life had changed somewhat. He kept getting waves of elation, and he patted the old black petrol tank lovingly as he put the bike onto its stand, but there was an underlying anxiety in him. A feeling that all was not going according to plan.

The thing with Allison had been a fiasco, and he blushed to recall it. She was such a sensible, dependable, loyal girl – and he was a bloody traitor, whichever way you looked at it. Tommy was his mate, his best mate along with Alan. His behaviour was unforgivable.

Tucker removed his helmet and began the walk across the concrete apron to the main door. Well anyway, she'd seen him off.

Allison had not exactly given Tucker a flea in his ear, but that was because she hadn't hung around. For the few seconds after he'd blurted out his idiocy, she'd just stared at him. Then she'd said: 'Tucker. Don't. You mustn't say that, you mustn't.'

Tucker had got himself into such a state that he'd forgotten to keep on blipping on the throttle, to keep the two-stroke burning and the plugs from oiling up. As Alli finished speaking, the engine stopped. Automatically, he looked down at it. A second later, when he raised his head, Allison was running down the street. He'd called, half-heartedly, 'Allison!', but she'd neither slowed down nor turned her head. He'd sat astride the bike for a good few minutes, pondering, before he'd kicked it back into action.

In the queue for Box Six, Alan and Tommy Watson were looking out for him. They'd clocked the crash-hat from ten yards away and they were jumping up and down like a pair of Mexican beans when he approached.

'Tucker! You tight bastard! You mean sod! You should be in the Masons, you should!'

Alan made a grab for the helmet, but Tucker pulled his arm away.

'The big secret!' said Tommy. 'I've got to give it to you, Tucker-son. Is it yours? What is it? When did you get it? It's never a Kawasaki?'

Alan added: 'Where did you get the loot, more to the point? Tucker – you haven't robbed a bank!'

Tommy had got his hands on the helmet. He'd given it the once-over.

'Piggy bank if he did, Al. Tucker, you ain't mugged a pensioner I hope? This lid's seen better days.'

Tucker had a flash of irrational rage.

'At least I've got one, Watson! What d'you expect, a BMW? I'm not a millionaire, you prat!'

Tommy dropped back, upset.

'Hey, come on, mate. I'm only bloody kidding you. Jesus, Tucker.'

Tucker was ashamed.

'Oh shit,' he said. 'Look, Tom.'

Alan cleared his throat theatrically.

'Gentlemen, gentlemen. If you're going to use foul language here, pray keep your voices low. They don't like to hear words like that, you know. It upsets them.'

The boys, relieved, rose to the diversion.

'Like what, you twat?'

'Like millionaire,' said Alan. 'And piggy bank and stuff. The trappings of high finance.'

'Bloody hell,' muttered the man behind them in the queue. 'And they give State benefits to morons like you. You wouldn't credit it.'

He was not being serious, however. They all shared a smile.

'Now come on, Tucker,' said Tommy Watson. 'What is it, and where did you get it from? Give us the bloody lowdown. Your secret's out.'

Tucker tried to enter into the spirit of things, but he just couldn't raise his level of enthusiasm. Tommy was all for leaving the queue, in relays, to go and have a look, and he was also determined to extract a promise from Tucker that he could have a go at the earliest possible opportunity.

'No,' said Tucker, flatly. 'Don't be so bloody daft, Tommy. You haven't even got a provisional.'

'Well, you could take me, then.'

'Look, that's against the law. You know it. And keep your rotten voice down. You never know who's lug'oling in this place.'

'Well they wouldn't get much to write to the Pope about out of you today,' said Tommy. 'What's the matter? If I'd got a bike I'd be over the moon. You're like a soggy gusset, you are. You're like a pimple on the p – '

They were close enough to Box Six for Medusa to take a hand. She cut in acidly: 'Will you please keep your voices down? And if there is any more obscenity I'll call the supervisor.'

After a pause for breath, Alan said quietly: 'You coming down the shop after, Tucker? We made a good start yesterday. We'd better get cracking again, all the time we can.'

'Nah,' said Tucker. 'I'm giving it a miss.'

'Hell,' said Alan. 'That's not fair. We've got to get it done. I should've thought you'd've been desperate for the –'

He broke off and coughed noisily. Medusa only inches away! He was going spare!

Tommy said: 'But if you're not coming, when do we get a go? We can't do it here, it's too busy. We could go to Alan's yard, afterwards.'

'You are *not* going to get a go.'

'You mingy twat,' said Tommy. You –'

'*Mister* Watson,' snapped Medusa. 'I will deal with you now, *if you stop* behaving like a lout.'

Tommy, tight-faced, turned away from Tucker. When he'd gone through the process he stamped off.

'I'll see you, Al,' he said. 'I'll meet you at the shop at two o'clock.'

'Mr Hargreaves, please,' said Medusa. Tucker looked at the yellow cord carpet. He blew a breath out through his lips.

Before Alan had finished going through the dreary business, Tucker was brought back to reality from his murky thoughts by a light tap on the shoulder. It was Michelle. He jumped.

'Oh, hello! Surprise surprise. What have you been up to?'

He thought perhaps he ought to peck her on the cheek, but he didn't want to. She made no move in that direction either, to his relief.

'Been across the JC,' she said. 'I thought I'd just pop over.'

'Ah,' said Tucker. 'We've been grafting down at –'

'Tucker,' she interrupted. 'What's that thing under your arm?'

Alan, who had finished with Medusa, was about to make a crack. He thought better of it, looking at Michelle's face. Gawd, he thought. It'll be a relief to be scrubbing up that paint today.

'See you, kids,' he said. He put on an American accent. 'Have a nice day!'

Some hopes.

'Well?' said Michelle.

'Mr Tucker,' said Medusa. 'You are late, of course – although less so than normal. Do you now intend to keep me waiting while you chatter? Some of us are very busy here.'

'Chance would be a fine thing,' said the man behind Tucker morosely. Medusa ignored it.

'Hold that,' said Tucker, thrusting the helmet at Michelle. 'It's a crash-hat, what did you think it was? I've got a motorbike.'

When Tucker had finished signing on, they moved to a quieter part of the hall to continue the conversation. Or the row. Michelle pushed the helmet back to Tucker as if it was poisonous.

'A motorbike,' she said. 'So you managed to persuade your Mum at last. Terrific. And how much is *that* going to cost you every week?'

'I'll manage,' Tucker answered. 'I thought you might be chuffed. I thought you might at least be interested.'

There was deep sarcasm in Michelle's voice.

'Oh, it's going to change my life!' she said. 'From now on, darling, everything's going to be just wonderful! The wind in my hair, the sun on my face, the faraway places we can visit at the drop of a hat. It'll be bliss, my handsome prince. Just bliss!'

You sarky cow, thought Tucker Jenkins.

'Well,' he said. 'It could be fun, at any rate.'

Michelle just looked at him.

'You haven't got a licence, have you, Jenkins? You've got L-plates up. You can't take me anywhere, and you know it. You haven't got the bottle to break the law in any case, I shouldn't wonder. But I wouldn't demean myself by making you.'

Ouch. Tucker was at a loss. Michelle was not.

'All that bike will mean to me,' she said, 'is that you'll have even less to spend on anything, if that was possible. What does it run on – toilet water? And after your little bust-up with my brother, you'll have bugger all to start with. You'll be broke as broke.'

'Hah!' said Tucker. 'I suppose your brother told you that, did he? Well you tell *him*, from *us*, that . . .' He stopped. How did Passmore know the damage he and Brains had done was going to cost them? Michelle soon answered that.

'I haven't seen my brother,' she said. 'I happened to bump into Tommy in a pub last night, that's all. We had a drink. He told me all about it. I think my brother –'

'What?' said Passmore's voice. Michelle and Tucker jumped. He walked casually from behind a screen, where he had obviously been listening. He stood before them, smiling easily, his peculiar hat perched on the back of his head. 'What do you think your brother? And what?' – to Tucker – 'would you like to tell me, little sweetheart?'

Michelle was disgusted.

'Oh for God's sake, Ralph,' she said. 'Just clear off and leave us, will you? Are you following me around? Are you out of your box, or something? This is a private matter.'

'Nothing's private between a brother and his sister,' he replied. 'I've told you before Michelle, I don't like that little tit.' He laughed contemptuously. 'That junior hell's angel there. Is that your bike parked near the fountain, Jenkins? The mighty one-two-five? I don't know how you handle all that naked power.'

'Look piss off, Ralph,' said Michelle. 'This is nothing to do with you.'

Passmore made a fist and moved it gently towards Tucker's face.

'Leave my sister alone, son.' he said quietly. 'Get out while the going's good. Yesterday was just rehearsals, a little bit of childish fun. I'm giving you fair warning. Leave my sister be.'

Michelle was white.

'You shut your bloody mouth,' she shouted. 'I'll go with anyone I want!'

An official in a suit was hurrying towards them. Not without apprehension. Everyone had stopped to watch. Passmore snapped his fingers under his sister's nose.

'I don't give that much for what you think,' he said. 'But nobody's going to call my sister a slag.'

He gave a loud bark of laughter.

'Except me!'

As the official reached them, he moved off.

'See you, Jenkins. See you, Mish.' He tipped the hat forward on his close-cropped skull.

'Separately, I hope,' he added. 'For both your sakes.'

It ended the row, at any rate. Tucker had been ready to give vent to his dark and secret feelings that Michelle was a gold-digger, who was only interested in him for what little cash he had and how she could get the benefit of it. Michelle was going to counter *her* supposed lack of inter-

81

est in the motorbike with *his* total lack of interest in what had happened at the Job Centre.

But by the time they'd calmed the benefit official down, they'd lost the impetus. He, of course – now that any real physical threat had passed with the departure of Ralph Passmore – came on very strong with them, and played the hard man for five minutes. When they left they did not make a date for that night, Michelle merely said she had something on. She did not even suggest she could come and view the bike. They kissed each other, coldly, briefly, and formally, and she walked away.

Tucker stood for a minute in the sunshine, deriving no pleasure from it at all. Phew, he thought. Do I remember feeling happy not so long ago? He caught sight of the bike over by the fountain. Black, beautiful, and his. His heart lifted. I'll go for a drive in the country. Thanks to good old Merve, I'm actually flush. I'll go and blue some petrol, I'll go and smell some grass, I'll go and pick some daisies for me mum!

As he got nearer, he could see something on the pavement by the bike. Something glinting in the sun. He stopped, then speeded up his pace. He stopped again two feet away, with his heart like lead. The glass from his headlamp was scattered on the paving stones and road.

Passmore, he thought, you're glorious. There goes my fifteen quid. And probably more besides.

The end of a perfect day.

Chapter Eleven

It was a couple of days before Tucker and Michelle, Allison and Tommy, got their act back together, and during these days the boys had worked hard and well together at the shop. The mess was cleared, the undercoating had been done, and the job would soon be over. Mr Hargreaves had forgiven them completely – although he hadn't let them off the hook financially, of course – and he'd hinted that he'd got a good, long-term task lined up, to do with fitting central heating in an old barn of a church hall.

Tucker had let them sit on the bike and fall in love with it, but he'd stuck to his guns over Tommy's wild desire to ride the thing. It didn't exactly cause the row to rumble on, because his argument was watertight. But Tommy did think he was being unnaturally – and uncharacteristically – careful of the law. Normally, Tucker would have risked it for a mate, no problem. But it was one of those things. Because of his confusion over Allison and everything, Tucker had got a sort of block on it. The bike was his alone. No one was to share.

He'd thought a lot about the Alli thing, and the more he'd thought the more ashamed he'd felt. The more foolish, too, because she'd shown no sign of giving a toss for him, let's face it. One passing reference to him looking sexy in a crash helmet and a couple of looks that could have meant *anything* – well, it was hardly the basis for a great romance . . . But it was shame, more than anything. He'd been a traitor to his mate. Or would have been, given half a chance.

Some of the banter at the shop still got home to him like red-hot knives, however. Talk from Tommy of what a goer Powell was, for instance. But he usually matched it with tales of him and Mish, when all was said and done, and he hadn't even kissed her properly for days! So maybe

Tommy, too . . . Alan didn't like the backchat either, it made him feel lonely and left out. Although the lads got plenty of time together, and still seemed more a unit than the boy/girl thing, he sometimes found himself at home alone at night, watching boring programmes on the box and pining after Susi. Still. He got quite miserable.

Tucker didn't mention it at work, but he had a plan on that score. His Mum and Dad were going off to Leicester in a while, and the house was going to be empty on a Friday night. All night. His Mum had only mentioned it to get a promise that he wouldn't wreck the joint by holding a party there, and Tucker had been forced to promise. But he'd thought about it since. A small select *soiree* perhaps. Just a few handpicked guests. No roughs, no scrubbers and no gatecrashers. If he handled it right, he'd be able to look her in the eye and say he'd kept his word.

The point was, it would kill two birds with one stone. It would be a little gesture to Tommy and Allison – and Michelle – to assuage his guilt at what he'd thought of doing, and it would be a chance to give Alan a laugh, get him out of himself, show him that they cared. Even, if it was remotely possible, maybe get a girl along for him, a friend of Allison's or Mish's. Well they must *know* other girls. And if it was not a party, more a dinner-do than a rave-up – well, what would be wrong with that?

To Tucker, who had no intention of telling Alan or the others that he'd planned all this on their behalf because he was such a wonderful human being, it looked flawless, the perfect plan. Everyone would be happy, and he'd be right with the world again. In a modest way, it gave him a warm glow inside at what a nice guy he was . . .

He did not mention it in front of Alan in case it did not work out, but most of all because he wanted to drop it in that night, at Tommy's flat. He'd arranged to meet Mish there, and he and Tom had split the beer-buying between them. Alan, luckily, was going off playing snooker at his old man's club, so that was no embarrassment. When Tucker rang the bell, his four-packs in his hand, he felt great. He'd even left the motorbike behind so that he could take Mish home.

Then Allison opened the door. And the first part of the masterplan began to crumble.

'Hi,' she said. 'I . . .'

Tucker was aware that he was going red.

'Oh! Allison. Oh . . . I . . .'

They were at a loss, both of them. Michelle came out of the sitting room door.

'Hi, Tucker,' she said, rather sourly. 'Forgotten your tin hat, have you? Don't say you've left your toy behind?'

Tucker stepped smartly in, smiling tightly at Allison. He thrust the four-packs into her hand.

'Shove them in the fridge while I get my jacket off, will you please? This ruddy central heating. It's too early in the year.'

'The heating isn't on,' said Mish. She went back into the sitting room.

Bloody Nora, thought Tucker. He watched Allison's back and bum and legs as she walked through to the kitchen. Every step she took seemed to tremble through the floor boards to his feet. And up his legs. Ow, he thought. Playing Mr Wonderful was not going to be a doddle, after all. No *way*.

Things did not get much better. First of all there was an argument with Debbie about shifting from the room. She claimed that she had the right to it because she had homework to do, and they were only there to mess about. This necessitated Mrs Watson being called from her bedroom where she was changing, and she cuffed Debbie's head. Then she stayed to chat to Allison, which embarrassed everybody rigid because she had so little on. She ended up by giving Tommy a lecture on being nice to his sister, but telling him to make sure she got to bed early, and belting her if she did not. Debbie screamed from the kitchen that she hated him, and hated her mum and hated everyone. There was a lot of tension in the air.

When the four of them sat down alone at last, Michelle stayed well clear of Tucker. Conversation did not happen. So Tucker, fed up but still with a certain amount of hope, dropped in the news.

'I'm thinking of having a party,' he said. 'I thought . . . I think we could do with cheering up.'

'Hey, great!' said Tommy. 'When?'

'But where?' asked Allison. 'Can we get a place?'

'We can!' said Tucker. 'We have! My mum and dad are going to me auntie's for the night. On a Friday, an'all. In a couple of weeks or so. I thought we could . . . I mean, we can . . . It'll be an all-night do.'

'Huh,' went Michelle. She had a look on.

'What's that meant to mean?' said Tucker. 'Come on, Mish, what's up? You don't seem even *interested*.'

Michelle looked at him levelly.

'That's what you said about your motorbike,' she replied. 'Down at the Dole House. Now it's about your party. Up at Tommy's flat. But *I'd* been to the JC, hadn't I? You never even asked me about that, I notice. I'm not the one who's not interested, Peter Jenkins.'

'What you on about?' said Tucker. 'You often go down the JC. We all do. Well, you know. We never get no jobs though, do we?'

Tommy smiled. It was a strange smile, as if he knew just what Mish was on about. As if they'd been talking.

'Ah,' he said. 'But Michelle got an interview, didn't she? And next week, Tucker, maybe she'll have a job!'

Tucker took in their expressions, puzzled.

'You mean *you* knew? Why didn't you tell me, you dumb prat?'

'Because I told him not to,' said Michelle. 'I wanted to see just how bloody long it would take you to find out. And it was too bloody long.'

Tucker tried to apologise, and tried to make it sound as if he meant it. But Michelle was unforgiving, and his patience was wearing pretty thin. When he tried to put his arm round her and she shrugged him roughly off, his temper flared. He kept it inside him, he moved casually away, but the effort nearly killed him. He sat down heavily on a chair and gritted his teeth.

After ten more lousy minutes, Michelle and Tommy decided to watch the film. They had no money to go out, and anyway, they had some beers in. Tucker made his decision.

'I'm going for a walk,' he said. 'I've seen the bloody film, and I'm not in the mood in any case.'

'A walk?' said Tommy. 'You're nuts. Where would you walk to?'

Allison said: 'There's lots of adverts in the newsagents down the road. You could look at them.'

It was such a weird suggestion that Michelle hooted with laughter.

'Don't tell him that, Allison,' she said sarcastically. 'He might find a job.'

Tucker grabbed his leather jacket from the back of a chair.

'Yeah,' he said. 'I might at that. I'm off.'

And Allison, as cool as an ice-cube, said: 'I think I'll come with you for the walk. I've seen the film, as well. You don't mind, do you Mish?'

'Why should I?'

'We won't be long,' said Allison. 'Tommy? You don't mind if I go out for a walk do you?'

'No,' said Tommy. 'I think you're loopy, but I don't mind. We'll watch the film.'

Tucker did not trust himself to speak.

They made a pretence of going to the newsagents, but the electricity in the air was so thick you could have run a freezer off it. Tucker did not dare come out with anything, just in case he'd got it all arse-upwards, but as they walked along they kept brushing against each other, then bouncing off. Surprise was that each contact wasn't signalled by a shower of sparks.

After they'd stood in front of the job cards for ten minutes, gulping silently, Tucker managed to say: 'Well.'

'Yeah,' said Allison. 'Well. Here we are.'

Tucker said: 'We'd better not be too long, I suppose.' He paused. 'Well, you know. They might suspect something.'

They both laughed nervously.

'What is there to suspect, though,' said Allison. 'I mean – we're all friends, aren't we? I mean, we're . . .'

'Yeah,' said Tucker. 'I suppose we'd better go then.'

With great reluctance, they headed back towards the flats. As they neared the entrance to the park it became ridiculous. Without either of them speaking, without any form of signal, they stopped by the gate.

'I suppose we could walk through here. It wouldn't take too long.'

'Yuh.'

In the end, they were sitting on a bench. The night was mild. The noise of London's traffic was subdued. You could see stars. Tucker sighed an enormous sigh.

'Allison,' he said. 'Do you remember what I said to you?'

He was conscious of the daftness of the question. But Alli did not laugh.

'Yeah,' she said. 'But Tucker. I'm meant to . . . I mean there's Tommy, and . . . and.'

'But do you want to . . . Do you feel . . . I mean.'

He moved towards her clumsily, almost taking her nose off with the cuff of his jacket. Allison dropped backwards, squirmed, got herself into the proper place. The first kiss, for Tucker, was like coming to the surface after drowning. It was more relief than anything. Just sheer, enormous, relief. It went on for a long, long time.

'Jesus Christ,' he said at last. 'I've wanted to do that for so long. Oh Allison. Oh, Jesus Christ.'

He moved in for another dose, but Allison pulled back.

'Oh Tucker,' she said. 'We mustn't, we mustn't. I'm going out with Tommy, and you're going out with Mish. This is wrong, Tucker, it's wrong.'

'We'll have to work it out,' he said. 'I know you're right, Alli, but we'll have to work it out. I think I . . . I said I love you, and I think I do. We'll have to work it out.'

Allison kissed him then, because there was something powerful in that, in hearing him say those words. They were so powerful that she almost felt the same, that she must love him too. But Tucker could detect the tenseness. He knew she was holding back. When he could bear to, he ended the kiss.

'You're right,' he said. 'I know you're being straight. I admire you for it Allison, I really do. But you do . . . want to, don't you? You do feel the same towards me . . . at least a little bit?'

This was easy, this was a relief.

'Oh yes,' said Allison. 'I think you're fantastic Tucker. I really, really like you. But . . . Well, well . . .'

'I know,' said Tucker. He wrapped her in his arms, but did not kiss her, feeling powerful, and honourable, and happy. They'd work it out, they'd have to. But in the meantime it was enough. To know she felt the same.

'We'd better go,' he said. 'We don't want the other two to worry, do we?'

'No. I wouldn't want to hurt them, Tucker. You understand that, don't you? I don't want anyone to get hurt.'

'You're fantastic,' said Tucker, adoringly. 'You're so incredibly *nice*.'

Back at the flat, when the doorbell rang, Tommy and Michelle practically destroyed themselves trying to get straight. Tucker and Allison had been away so long that they'd assumed they'd gone for good. In fact, they'd forgotten all about them. When Debbie hammered on the sitting room door then pushed it open they were almost back to rights. But there was no point in pretending about what had been going on. No point at all.

Tucker switched the main light on and stood stock still. To his *greater* surprise, he was hurt. He felt as if someone had kicked him in the guts.

'You bastard, Watson,' he said. 'You lousy, two-timing, stinking little shit!'

Allison sat down on a chair without a word. If she was upset she did not show it. Tommy, on the contrary, looked bowled over.

'I'm sorry, Tuck,' he mumbled. 'It was – I mean. Oh, Christ, man.'

'Oh stop drivelling,' snapped Michelle. She did the last button of her blouse up and took a swig of beer from a can. 'What do you think *he's* been up to, stupid? Come on, Tucker. Come on, Allison. Just where the hell have *you* been all this time?'

'Now look here, Mish,' stormed Tucker. He stopped suddenly. There was a funny noise behind him. It was Debbie, in the doorway, trying to stifle the most massive fit of giggles. She was hanging on the doorpost, with her legs crossed.

'You sod off up to bed, our kid,' yelled Tommy Watson. 'I'll give you such a hammering!'

But the spell was broken. Debbie became paralysed with giggles. She fell to the ground, squawking and rolling about. They watched her in growing amazement and concern.

'Perhaps she needs a doctor,' said Allison.

Tucker was losing his control. Great waves of giggles were pushing up his chest.

'Perhaps she needs a vet!'

Debbie was sick in the end, but she'd enjoyed it. All five of them ended up in a typhoon of laughter. When Debbie made herself ill Tommy mopped her down and Mish helped her into bed.

Tucker and Allison took that opportunity to leave. It was quite a romantic night, with lots of stars and a moon. But they were still giggling when they kissed goodnight.

Chapter Twelve

Over the next couple of weeks, everything seemed perfect for the foursome – although Alan took the news of the switchover quite badly, in a quiet way. What sort of dead-head must he be, he wondered, if everyone else was so super-sexy that they couldn't keep their hands off each *other's* birds and blokes, let alone their own? But he tried not to show it, and they tried not to let him see they felt sorry for him.

They did though, and once the new 'grouping' had been settled into, they called a conference on the party scheme. Michelle, naturally, was no longer anti it, in fact she could hardly wait. She seemed keener still when Tucker said it had to be a quiet 'refined' affair because of problems with his Mum and Dad. The idea of a sophisticated dinner-do, with low lights and soft music maybe, appealed to her.

'One thing, now I'm going out with Tommy,' she laughed. 'I won't be ashamed to be seen with him in company. He's got some clothes sense, not like you, Tucker.'

'He's got some *clothes*,' retorted Tucker. 'What you expecting then, Mish? White tie and tails? It won't be as quiet as *all* that!'

'So how many exactly do you reckon on having?' said Allison. The four of them were in a coffee bar, and she was pressed up close and loving. Allison liked his leather and jeans look, it was dead butch. Tommy, now, seemed overdressed to her, too finicky.

'I don't know yet,' said Tucker. 'It depends on all sorts of things. Like how much cash we've got, and who's going to cook it if we eat, and if we can afford wine, and that. Proper wine, I mean, to go with food. Can any of you two cook?'

Mish and Allison swapped glances. Oi oi, they'd heard this one before.

'Look, Peter Jenkins,' said Michelle. 'If it's an eating do, we buy it in. We get a classy takeaway or something. We are *not* your wives or mothers, right?'

'Yeah,' said Allison. 'Haven't you ever heard of the sexual revolution, Tucker?'

'Course I have,' he said. 'It's doing it on a roundabout!'

It was good fun talking it over, all the same, and they planned and plotted for ages, without getting very far. Tucker raised the question of Alan rather delicately for him, he thought.

'What about Al?' he said. 'Can we dig up some crumpet for him to bring along? That'd be ace.'

'Tucker!' went Michelle. 'You're so *gross*. I can't imagine what I ever *saw* in you!'

Allison kissed his ear.

'His suaveness and sensitivity I expect,' she said. 'He's famous for it.'

'Yeah,' said Tommy. 'In some of the best doss-houses in town!'

'Listen, cut the comedy for a minute, I'm being serious. What *can* we do for Al? If we *could* arrange a girl for the night it'd be terrific.'

'For the night!' Allison put on her wide-eyed look. Tucker smacked her lightly on the cheek.

'Be *serious*. The poor sod's suffering. He's still holding a candle for that miserable cow Susi McMahon, God knows why. She's as much laughs as a barbed wire bellyband. *Could* we set him up?'

Tommy nodded.

'Just for the night, like. You know, a sort of blind date. A one-off. Just to cheer him up.'

'She'd have to be blind,' Michelle said.

'Well you went with Tucker!'

Allison was scratching her cheekbone, thoughtfully. Ideas time.

'Well I *might*,' she said. 'There's just an outside chance that my cousin Andrea wou –'

'Andrea!' whooped Tucker. 'You must be joking! What sort of name is that?'

'Suit yourself,' said Allison. 'If you don't like someone

just because of their name it's no skin off my nose.'

'But what's she like?' asked Tommy. 'With a monicker like that she must be a right dog, is she?'

The girls could hardly believe it. These boys were Stone-agers.

'I wonder what they talk about us like, behind our backs,' said Mish. 'A right dog! You'd think that Women's Lib had never bloody happened. You just tell this Andrea what they said, Alli. That should put the kybosh on, good and proper.'

They got it sorted in the end, though, and the boys ate humble pie for Alan's sake. Also for Alan's sake, Alli said she'd speak to Andrea, although she didn't sound too hopeful. They split up happily, arranging to meet later on that night.

Left alone, the girls got to chatting about their respective fellers. It was a funny position they were in, the way they'd swapped. But Michelle, who wasn't noted for her tact, got the ball rolling.

'I really *can't* see why I fancied Tucker,' she said. She sipped her new cup of coffee. 'He really is a lunk. Tommy's a much better dresser. And he's got more cash to spend.'

'Well, now Tucker's got the motorbike, I suppose,' admitted Allison. 'But I don't care. I don't care about the jacket and those jeans, either. He's nice, I think. He's dead intelligent, and he's . . . well, like I said – sensitive.'

'If not exactly suave!' said Mish. 'Yeah, maybe you're right. To be quite honest, Alli, I like a bit more suaveness in a bloke. Tommy takes care of himself, he's always at the mirror, he wants to look good for a girl. And if he's got anything, even a few bob, he'll spend it. There's a careful streak in Tucker I don't like. He's capable of saving for a motorbike, fine. But that didn't make *me* feel very important. Tommy Watson treats me as more important than a motorbike.'

'Yeah, but Tucker's . . . tougher, sort of. Harder. Tommy's pretty easy to . . . lead. It's never hard to get your way with him.'

'Lovely,' said Michelle. 'That suits me, Alli. I love a

93

man I can wind around my little finger. I think Tommy needs a tough woman to look after him. And I'm tough!'

'Oh I like to be . . .' Allison tailed off, blushing slightly. She'd been going to say 'dominated' but that sounded wrong, tacky. She changed it in mid-sentence. 'I like to be with someone sort of . . . serious, you know. I think Tucker would respect my wishes more. I want to be a nurse, I want to get my O-levels, not mess about *too* much. I think Tucker agrees with that. Tommy just thinks having a good time's what's most important.'

'My brother's tough,' said Michelle. 'Is that why you fell for him? Did you love him? Do you love Tucker?'

Too many questions – and the wrong ones! Allison was scarlet. Ralph Passmore did not fit in with the dream. He did not understand her insistence on work, and passing exams, and getting on. He was tough all right, he was dominant. And exciting too, rebellious, dangerous and exciting. But he frightened her, and because of him the very thought of love was frightening. Did she love Tucker? No. If she loved anyone it was . . . But she could not. She must not get involved, she must deny it. To herself and everyone.

She said in a faint voice: 'You must think I'm very shallow, Mish.'

Michelle looked back at her in total bewilderment.

'Shallow?' she asked. 'What are you on about?'

Alan's state of mind got so bad gradually, that Mr Hargreaves took the step of mentioning it to Tucker and Tommy Watson, and asking if there was anything that could be done.

'It's that Susi girl,' he said. 'They say that love is blind. What he needs is some young dumpling with a good strong back for a week or two. He's over eleven stone you know, it's terrible. Other kids get acne if they don't have their oats. I'd rather that than have him exploding up a ladder one day. The fall-out would be incredible.'

They were in the yard getting everything ready for the central heating job. It was a big one, and it had caused a fair amount of friction. There were dozens of radiators to be humped, and miles of old lead piping to be cleared, and various other heavy, dirty and unpleasant tasks. Tucker had suggested more than once that they should get a rise for it, especially as they were being asked to do work that was at least semi-skilled, and required concentration and intelligence. He had got nowhere.

'If you don't like it, my son, you can go,' Mr H had said. He knew about the new financial bind, with the bike. He knew he had them by the short and curlies. They'd had a couple of mini-rows, and this friendly chat was an exception, no longer just the rule. Alan was down the plumbing supply firm, sorting out the latest consignment of parts.

'Well as it happens,' said Tommy Watson, 'we have got a plan, Mr H. Young Tucker here – '

'At vast expense,' put in Tucker, meaningfully.

'Has organised a party. Don't tell Alan yet, but it should be one hell of a do. And we might, we just *might* – '

'Ask you for a small donation,' finished Tucker.

He didn't mean it, he knew Mr H too well. But it hadn't seemed right to mention the girl. For all his joking about acne, Mr H might take that quite badly. To his amazement, Mr Hargreaves reached into his back pocket. He took his wallet out.

'You're nice boys, the pair of you,' he said. 'I'm going to put a fiver in.'

Tucker, open-mouthed, reached out his hand. Mr H's eyes narrowed. The wallet hovered. Then snapped shut.

'I'll tell you what,' he said. 'Ask me when it's definite.'

'It *is* definite!' said Tommy. 'Ain't it, Tuck?'

'Of course it is,' said Tucker. He beamed at Alan's dad. 'Thanks Mr H,' he said. 'You had me worried there for a second at least. You've reaffirmed my faith in human nature. You *are* a mean old twat.'

Mr Hargreaves stuffed his wallet back into safe keeping. He leered.

'And you're a cheeky one. But I mean it, boys. You're good lads, and I'll put a fiver in. Now – get your bloody fingers out, the pair of you.'

* * *

That dinnertime, with his two mates off to see their girls as usual, Alan found himself drifting, on a tide of futility, to the college where the object of his dreams would be. He treated his need to go, his inability to stay away, with a strange degree of self-disgust, considering. He knew it was stupid, he knew he was ridiculous. And he knew that if he saw her it would only increase his humiliation and his shame.

He'd got so sensitive to the absurdity of his own actions, that he imagined, when he got there, that all the students recognised him. He stood at the corner of a building, dodging every now and then behind a stone pillar, his expression ranging from blank to embarrassed. Some of the kids in jeans and scarves did smile at him, but he only managed to smirk hideously back, convinced that they were laughing.

Alan had been there for ten minutes when he spotted Susi. She came out of the main building, her ash-blonde, curly hair gleaming in the sun. The sight of her would have been pain enough, but she was not alone. She was with a feller, and they were holding hands.

Like a rabbit fascinated by a snake, Alan could not move. He recognised the boy as one he'd seen with Susi McMahon before. It was clearly her new bloke, steady, regular. He hoped that he would be invisible to them until they had gone. He was suffering all right, but he knew that it was his problem, no one else's. He wanted to suffer in silence, on his tod.

Susi spotted him. The smile froze on her face. She looked at the bloke, nodded towards Alan, and said something. He looked at Alan, then said something to Susi. She kissed his cheek, let go of his hand, and walked over. She did not look friendly.

'Oh,' said Alan. 'Hi, Susi. I was just – '

'Look Alan,' said Susi. 'Piss off will you? I'm getting fed up of this.'

'I was only passing. I – '

'Shut your mouth,' she said angrily. 'I'm tired of it, right? That's my feller over there, and he's all for punching your face in. If you hang around here any more I'll let him, right?'

Alan said nothing. He moved his hand in a vague gesture.

'Did you get that?' snapped Susi. 'I'm sick to death of you hanging round me, Alan. I won't bloody stand for it. Do you get that?'

When it became obvious that he would not reply, Susi turned away. She stalked back to her bloke.

'I'm warning you, that's all,' she said. 'I'm warning you.'

Back at the yard after dinner, Tucker and Tommy could hardly wait to tell Alan the news. The fact that he appeared as miserable as they'd ever seen him only made it better. Tucker opened up as they piled into the back of the pick-up.

'You miserable lump of lard,' he said jovially. 'You'd make a statue weep you would. What's up with you?'

'Sod off,' said Alan.

'You need cheering up,' said Tommy. 'So pin your ears back and listen to this, old son. Tucker's having a party. In *your* honour!'

For a moment, interest flickered.

'When?'

'Friday week. Me Mum and Dad are off to Leicester.'

Tommy said: 'Soft lights, smoochy music, champagne, caviar – and crumpet!'

A black shutter fell in Alan's brain. He jumped to the ground off the back of the truck.

'Yeah,' he said. 'That's right, innit? Two mates, two girls, and *me*. No crumpet for fat Alan, is there? No crumpet's thick enough to *bother*!'

'But Al!' said Tucker. He couldn't mention Andrea. Nothing had been finalised.

'It's in your honour,' said Tommy. 'Your dad – '

'Balls to me dad,' said Alan. 'And balls to you. I'm not coming to your crummy party, and I'm not working this afternoon. Balls to the lot of you.'

He was away. He shot through the yard, through the back door, and that was that.

'Christ,' said Tucker.

Chapter Thirteen

Setbacks never come singly, and in the days after Alan's refusal to play lapdog at the party, things fell apart with amazing speed. The friction between Tucker and Mr Hargreaves broke into a row, Michelle got a job that caused more trouble than it was worth, and Allison and Tucker had their first bust-up over money. By the time Tommy got his hands on Tucker's motorbike, things were ripe for a disaster.

The root of it all, stupidly enough, was the party. After the incident at the yard, Tucker and Tommy Watson took every possible opportunity to nag at Alan to change his mind, which made him more and more stubborn about it. Tucker, desperate for something to beat him into submission with, put strong pressure on Allison to persuade Andrea, and fast, until she accused him of trying merely to use her and other people. Then the cost reared its ugly head.

Michelle, at the beginning of the week, was as happy as a dog with two tails. On the Monday morning, she'd had a call from the food factory where she'd had the interview. The person who'd been given the job had never turned up – so could she? Could she ever! She'd started the very next morning, and she'd been full of herself. The trouble was, she'd not been able to keep from making the odd sarky remark about 'real' jobs for 'real' wages; and Tucker had equally stupidly made a crack about sticking cherries onto cakes on a conveyor belt not being his idea of a 'real' job.

Tommy had jokingly sided with Tucker, Allison had thought they were a pair of pigs, and a reference to the enormous cost of the party and how Mish would be able to pay her share of something at last had set another ball rolling. In the end even Allison and Tucker had been snarling at each other over money, which she said he squandered and he said she had no right to comment on as she had none herself, only being a schoolkid. It had guaranteed a frosty night for all of them.

They'd patched it up all right, but the next morning at the yard Tucker, yet again, had tackled Mr H about more cash for the heating job.

'Look, Tucker,' said Alan's dad. 'I've told you once and I've told you twice. I can't pay you any more, because I can't afford to. I am *not* a millionaire and I am *not*, whatever you think, a bloated capitalist.'

'But our labour on this job is saving you a fortune. You can't deny it.'

'I wouldn't even bother. If I was paying proper wages, you stupid sod, I wouldn't've been able to take it on. Can't you understand that?'

'So you're trying to tell me you won't make a big fat profit on it, are you?'

They were standing by the pick-up, and it was so early in the day that Tucker still had his crash-hat in his hand. He'd just hauled the bike onto its stand.

'I'm not trying to tell you anything about my profits. They're none of your bloody business. Now where's that Tommy Watson? I want to fetch some cement for the Erskine Road job. I need someone who can hump sacks without boring my arse off all the time.'

'So you're refusing to discuss it, are you?'

Mr Hargreaves looked squarely at Tucker.

'Listen, son,' he said. 'If you call this a discussion you're a bigger fool than I take you for. I'm prepared to talk about it rationally if you are. If you're prepared to listen to what I say and not just think I'm lying. Think about it.'

Tucker looped the crash helmet over the handlebars as Tommy arrived. Then Alan came out of the house.

'Right,' said Mr Hargreaves. 'One volunteer to help me fetch cement. The other two to stay here and sort out the copper piping. Which?'

'I'll come,' said Tucker. 'I'd like to talk.'

'Wahee!' mocked Tommy. 'You two in love, are you!'

'You heard what I said?' asked Mr Hargreaves.

'Yeah,' replied Tucker. 'Rational chat. I'm fed up with all this rowing.'

'Good. So am I.'

When they'd driven off, Alan nodded to the kitchen.

'The lord and master's left the list of pipes to sort in there,' he said. 'Shall we read it over a cup of tea?'

But Tommy Watson was gazing at Tucker's bike.

'Look,' he said. 'D'you know what the silly bugger's done? He's only left the key in!'

An expression of alarm crossed Alan's face.

'Here, leave it out, Tom. You ain't going to touch it, are you?'

'Well, the tight sod,' said Tommy 'We are his bloody mates. I've never known him be so mingy over anything.'

'Yes,' said Alan. 'We are his *mates*, Tommy. And mates don't nick other mates' motorbikes, do they?'

Tommy sneered. He patted the crash helmet.

'You can be such an old woman, Al. I'm not going to do it any harm. I'll just start it up. Go for a little potter round the yard.'

There was no room in the yard, they both knew that. Once he'd started it, it would be a spin around the roads. Alan shook his head.

'You haven't got a licence. You haven't got insurance. If a copper stopped you, you'd be finished. It would cost you a fortune. An arm and a leg.'

But the bike was already off the stand. The curly head of Tommy Watson was disappearing into the crash helmet. The key was turned, the starter kicked.

Tommy, astride the bike, grinned at Alan and gave the thumbs up sign.

'Chocks away!'

'You're stupid,' muttered Alan. He breathed in the aromatic smoke, then turned for the kitchen. 'Stupid.'

Tommy had never owned a bike, but he'd ridden them a couple of times. After a wobbly start, in the road outside the yard, he got the feel of it quickly enough. He stayed away from the busy places, and he waited an unnaturally long time crossing junctions. Once, he passed a motorcycle cop, and he almost froze with fear. But he puttered past safely and sedately, and the policeman hardly glanced at him.

It was great, it was lovely, it was wonderful. Tommy thought about the money moans of the night before, when even Allison had made a reference to Tucker's bike being a luxury he could not afford. Girls were mad. What could be more important than a thing like this? It wasn't luxury, it was life! It was the bare necessity for existence!

Inevitably, Tommy's plan to be away from the yard for five or ten minutes came to nothing. He did not look at his watch, and he was unaware of the passage of time. It occurred to him, very suddenly, that he'd been gone too long. It occurred to him when he realised he was a good fifteen minutes ride away from Alan's house.

He began to hurry. He began to drive faster than he should have done. He began to panic slightly. What would Tucker say if he got back before him? What the hell would Tucker say?

Tucker and Mr Hargreaves were not far from the yard by now, and Tucker was saying nothing. The 'rational talk' had lasted for ten minutes or so, and then deteriorated. They'd had a full-scale row over the cement sacks, and they were riding along in silence. They turned right onto the canal-side road leading to the yard as Tommy drove along it.

Tucker, looking left, saw him coming.

'Jesus Christ!'

He wound the window down so fast he nearly tore the handle off.

'Watson!' he roared. 'What the – '

Tommy Watson heard, looked, and fell to pieces. The bike bounced over the low kerb off the road, and headed for the canal. Tommy got control and shot off down the towpath. Until he met an angler, under a vast green sun-umbrella. The angler, terrified, jumped to his feet and to the right, shouting. Tommy headed left, hopelessly. He thought unmentionable thoughts as the murky waters folded over him.

When he rose to the surface seconds later, the unmentionable thoughts had been replaced by even more unmentionable descriptions of what should happen to him. Tucker was on the bank above him, dancing with rage and

101

shouting obscenely. Tommy stepped backwards farther into the soft mud of the canal. It seemed the safest thing to do.

Despite Tucker's repeated – and apparently serious – suggestion that they leave him there to drown, Tommy Watson was finally pulled out. If Tucker had not been restrained by both Mr Hargreaves and the fisherman, there would undoubtedly have been a fight. Because Tommy, having nothing at all to say in his own defence, tried attack.

'You bloody moron,' he told Tucker. 'You could have killed me then, you fool. Shouting out like that. I'm lucky to be alive.'

Tucker was on the borderline between fury and tears for several minutes. He was convinced the bike was ruined. All that was left of it was the odd bubble and a patch of iridescent oil on the surface of the water. Its insides would rust to pieces in seconds. Its electrics would be shot. He told Tommy to go, to disappear, to get away while the going was good. Mr Hargreaves intervened.

'Look, Tucker,' he said. 'You've had your shout, all right? Now shut your row up and listen. If you want to save that bike, my son, we've got to get it out of there. Fast. And for that we need Tommy. He's wet already. He can go down and get a rope on it, pronto.'

'What's the use?' said Tucker. 'Leave it there. It's finished.'

'No you don't!' said the fisherman. 'What about pollution? What about the fish?'

Mr Hargreaves pulled Tucker away before he could make any suggestions about the fish. He dragged the pair of them towards the truck.

'If we're quick,' he said. 'We'll be all right. We'll whip it out, we'll get out the plugs, drain the cylinders and exhaust pipe, strip down the magneto, oil everything, dry it off, and get it going. It's a motorbike, Tucker, it's not a piece of priceless microbleedingelectronics. If we shift, we can save it.'

Tucker did not believe him, but he apparently was not joking. Five minutes later they had the bike out and standing on its back wheel to drain. Then they put it in the truck.

'Right,' said Mr H. 'You've got a day off, Tucker. On me. Let's get it to the workshop so that you can start. There's all the tools there. All you've got to do, son, is move fast, and be thorough. I'll give you a hand.'

Bloody hell. People were a mystery . . .

In the middle of the day, Tucker phoned Allison's house to tell her he'd be late that night. They were meeting outside a cinema, with a view to going in if the mood took them and if the cash situation was good enough. They always met away from her home because she had trouble with her father over boys. He did not like them.

Tucker was rather dismayed when her father answered, but he did not have much choice. Allison was not there, and even if she had been her dad would not have put her on. Tucker gave his message and hung up. For a while he felt worried about whether she'd be told, but he soon became absorbed in saving the bike. By teatime, he was making progress. If all went well – if the bike actually worked again – he'd only be half an hour late or so in any case. He worked on.

Allison had been waiting for more than twenty minutes when Ralph Passmore came along, and by then she was seriously wondering if Tucker had stood her up. She ignored Ralph when he said Hello, and raised her pert little nose into the air. He laughed at her, and wandered on. But he did not go far.

Allison cast her mind back rather frantically to the night before. Had they had a row, exactly? It had all been very tense, but surely it had ended up all right? Tucker had walked her home, and they had lots of kissing at the end of the street. Surely he wouldn't have left her standing because of all that stuff earlier?

But she *had* been left standing. She looked at her watch, feeling frustrated and angry. And then she thought – oh well, maybe I am to blame. Maybe I am a mean cow sometimes.

103

In her handbag, Allison had two quid which she'd borrowed off her mum to spend tonight. As a gesture, for the row. Because although Michelle nagged at her, she didn't like to make a fuss over who paid what for whom. She didn't expect to be treated every time. She didn't expect Tucker to give up his part time job and go mad to find a 'real' one. She didn't even think he spent too much on the bike. Except sometimes. When Michelle nagged at her.

But then again . . . Allison glanced at her watch once more, feeling furious. She must look such a *fool* standing there. So *obviously* waiting for someone. So *obviously* having been stood up. It was unforgivable.

'Hello again.'

It was Passmore. He stood in front of her with his threatening smile and his extraordinary hat. She knew what he was going to say. He'd make some snidy reference to the fact that she'd been left in the lurch.

He did not.

'It's a nice night for a little walk and a talk,' he said. 'It's a nice night for a little drink. What a pity you're tied up.'

'I'm not,' she said. And shocked herself.

His smile became less threatening, more humorous.

'Tied down, I mean,' he laughed.

All the old confusions crowded Allison's mind. He could be so terrific, Ralph. He could be such a nice, funny, kind guy. And there was no rubbish about money. If he had it they spent, if he didn't they didn't. And she couldn't deny, to herself, that she still thought he was dead good-looking. So *amazingly* tough.

'Not tied down either,' she said. She had a squirm of panic and betrayal in her stomach. Oh Tucker, Tucker!

'I'm pleased to hear it,' said Passmore, easily. 'I'm at a loose end myself tonight. Fancy coming for a quiet drink with me? For old times sake?'

Allison's mouth was so dry she could hardly reply. What's going *on*, she thought. Just what am I *doing*?

'Yeah, all right,' she said. 'Just a little one.'

'Good,' he smiled. 'Come on, then.'

Tucker turned up ten minutes later, on the bike. He was disappointed that she was not there, but not too put down. The bike was saved. It was going like a bomb.

She must have gone back home. To watch the boring telly with her boring dad and mum. He'd get in touch tomorrow. He'd meet her at the school.

Tucker went off for a celebration drive. He felt he'd really achieved something today . . .

Chapter Fourteen

Funnily enough, it was Alan who had a great time for the rest of the week, and it got up the noses of the other two more than somewhat. It came about through Allison, and it changed his mind about the party in one short, sharp stroke.

Tucker took the news to him after quite a difficult session with Alli the next dinner hour. He turned up outside school on the bike as he often did, and parked conspicuously in the usual place. But Allison did not come out.

After he'd been standing for about ten minutes, Tucker wandered into the schoolyard in the hope of meeting Debbie Watson or someone else he knew. But he didn't have to – because he spotted Allison standing inside the entrance hallway, talking to a friend.

'Hi,' he said. 'I've been waiting for you outside. What's up?'

Allison looked strained, and she was wearing a chiffon scarf round her neck. Tucker indicated it.

'What's the fancy collar for? You'll get detention, you will!'

The other girl gave Allison a look.

'I've . . . cut my neck,' said Allison. She pulled the scarf down to reveal a plaster. 'I've got permission.'

'Well can't you come outside?' said Tucker. 'I want to talk to you.'

Allison seemed unsure of what to do. Then she shrugged.

'All right,' she said. 'Look, Pam, I'll see you later, right?'

'Yeah,' said Pam. 'Tara. Mind you don't cut yourself shaving again!'

Giggling, she moved off. Tucker and Allison went into the street.

'Strange girl,' said Tucker. 'How *did* you cut –'

'Look, Tucker,' said Allison. 'Where the heck *were* you last night? I waited and waited. You made me look a proper fool. I could've got *raped*.'

'Oh my God,' said Tucker. 'D'you mean to say your dad didn't tell you? What a – '

'Tell me what?' Her voice had gone small.

'I had a smash-up on the bike. Well, Tommy did. The silly bugger borrowed it and drove it in the canal. I had to spend about ten hours fixing it. I made it go. Me and Mr Hargreaves. I rang you up.'

'Oh,' said Allison. 'Was . . . was Tommy hurt?'

'He bloody should've been,' said Tucker. 'It was only Mr Hargreaves kept me off of him. I'd've drowned him given half a chance, the prat. But what about your father, eh? I've a damn good mind to ring him up!'

'No!' said Allison. 'Don't be stupid!'

'But it must've wrecked your evening. What did you do? Watch TV? How *did* you cut your neck?'

Allison was very flustered.

'It's a sort of bruise,' she said. 'Not so much a cut. I did it . . . washing up. A glass broke.'

'What, and bruised you? How?'

'A cup . . . Sort of heavy earthenware. Oh Tucker, don't go on. Listen – ' Her face brightened. 'I forgot to tell you. Andrea got in touch. She rung this morning because I wasn't – Because she missed me last night. It's on! She's coming to the party. For Alan.'

'Hey, that's great!' said Tucker. 'That'll make him change his tune! Look, we'll need to talk about the details, then. We've only got three or four days. Let's organise a meeting at Tommy's, the five of us. Tomorrow night say. Give Mish time to sort herself out if she's busy.'

'No,' said Allison. 'Not tomorrow night. I'm tied up then. I've got to . . . it's my . . . it's a family thing. It'll have to be tonight. Or the day *after* tomorrow, maybe.'

'Oh come on! That'd only give us one clear evening Can't you – '

'Look, Tucker Jenkins,' said Allison, snappily.

'Whoops! *Soh*ree!' He said it in a sing-song, comic voice. 'No, I just can't wait, that's all. Sorry.'

'Hmm,' said Allison. She checked her watch. 'I want some dinner. You'd better go. I'll see you after school.'

Tucker hung about, wanting to say something. She got impatient.

'Come on, Tucker. I want to go. What's eating you?'

'It's . . . I mean . . . Look, Alli. I know you'll be angry if I say this but . . . Well, Andrea's *not* a dog, is she? She's not . . .'

'You're disgusting, you are! If someone talked about a boy like that, one of your friends!'

'Yeah, I know, Alli. But –'

'Oh shut up, Tucker. You make me sick,' she said. And she stomped back into the playground without a backward glance.

God, she thought. What a mess. She touched the plaster on her neck, under the chiffon.

God, thought Tucker. What if she is an ugly crow? What would *that* do to poor old Alan?

'Poor old Alan' had a lovely afternoon, even if his mates did not. When Tucker told him, at the end of dinnertime, he almost turned cartwheels.

'A blind date!' he said. 'You daft buggers!' he said. 'What's she like?' he said.

He gave a burst of laughter.

'I hope she's not some manky old boot!' he chirruped. 'I hope I don't have to wear dark glasses and pretend I'm blind! You daft buggers!'

'Well,' said Tucker cautiously. 'I've never actually seen her, Al. But she's Alli's mate. She's her cousin, I think. Alli wouldn't pull no tricks, would she?'

Tommy said, rather sourly: 'I take it from your happy smiling face that you're coming after all?'

'Course I am,' said Alan. 'I was coming anyway. I just didn't want you to think I was no pushover!'

They pushed him over properly at that, and they were larking about when Mr Hargreaves came out of the house.

'I hope you've got your wellies and your overalls,' he said. 'We've got a rush job on.'

Despite them nagging, he would not tell them what it

was until they reached a big suburban house some miles away. In the back garden was an evil-smelling pool of bubbling filth.

'Drains?' said Alan. 'You rotten sod, Dad. We're not digging drains, surely to God?'

Mr Hargreaves laughed, but no one else did. Tucker was furious.

'Bloody hell, Mr H! We're not sewage labourers, you know. You need special gear for this. We'll get filthy. Our clothes'll reek of it. *And* I suppose you're offering your usual bugger all as bonus?'

'Oh come on, lads,' said Alan's dad. 'It's a rush job. An emergency. I can't afford to turn jobs down, you know.'

'Right,' said Tucker. 'If it's a rush job, we'll have a rush job rate.'

'Yeah,' said Tommy. Alan looked rebellious.

'Oh that's very nice,' said Mr H. 'That's wonderful, that is. When did the bike go in the drink, Tucker? Only yesterday was it, son? And who put it there, Tommy?'

He looked from one to the other of them.

'And who got *both* of you out of the shit? As a *rush* job?'

Tucker and Tommy were silenced. Alan said quietly: 'That's not the point, Dad.'

'Oh I'm sick of you,' said Mr Hargreaves. 'I'm going to get the gear out of the truck. If you don't want to give me a hand, don't. But it's a long walk home.'

They stood about for a minute or two, as a gesture, then joined in. But from time to time, as they dug and podged among the evil, stinking slurry, they muttered to each other of strikes and suchlike. For Tucker, things were coming to a head.

They were for Tommy also, in a different way. A couple of hours later, he was standing up a ladder. Below his face was the inspection hatch to a four-inch soil pipe, open. The other three were in the garden, puzzling over why the drains were still not running when they should be free.

'It may be a pressure blockage,' Mr Hargreaves mused. 'A gas build-up. If we've done it right, it should have – Oh my Gawd!'

There was a bilious rumbling sound within the piping at their feet.

'Tommy!' shouted Mr H. 'Mind your bleeding face!'

Too late. As Tommy moved his head back, a puff of filthy air shot from the hatch. Closely followed by a thick spray of brown and lumpy waste. He was covered in it.

The three of them stood watching him, awed into silence.

'The poor bastard,' said Alan. 'He can't even open his mouth to scream . . .'

Tommy was in fact too shaken and revolted to do much at all. When the others had finished laughing they cleaned him off as best they could. They filled in the hole, tested the system, and got back in the truck. Tommy was made to sit alone, downwind.

Mr Hargreaves drove him to the flats, and when Tommy was on the pavement with him, he got his wallet out.

'There you are,' he said. 'There's a tenner. I know we laughed, Tom, but I'm sorry. You'll need a new shirt at least.'

'I need a bath,' said Tommy. 'That's what I really need. But thanks, Mr H. I appreciate that.'

'Don't forget the conference, Tom,' said Tucker. 'We'll be round at eight o'clock. We'll bring our own clothes-pegs for our noses, don't you bother.'

After he'd gone, Tucker leaned out of the back.

'By the way,' he said. 'It's the party on Friday, Mr H. Definite. How about that five you promised us?'

Mr Hargreaves' jaw dropped. Then he grinned ruefully.

'You win, Tucker,' he said. 'You bloody pirate you.'

For the boys – and Alan in particular – the party was terrific. Although it didn't turn out to be a brawl, precisely, it was hardly the quiet soirée they'd originally talked about. Somehow the news leaked out, and somehow a few mates drifted along. Not gatecrashers – it turned out that they'd been invited sort of, vaguely, in a way. And they all brought bottles, and some of the girls brought pies, and bits of cheese, and fancy salads in

110

dishes. They didn't blow the walls out with the noise, but it wasn't the tea lounge at the Grand Hotel, either. It was a good party.

Andrea, who turned up at a stage where Alan was about to die of nerves, was great. If she wasn't a raving beauty, she was by no means out of the hunt. Alan had dressed himself up to the nines, like a dog's dinner, and combed his hair so often he'd probably go prematurely bald. His clothes tended to the slightly formal and old-fashioned, which suited Andrea well. She was a big, dark-haired girl in a print dress, who seemed to enjoy eating, drinking and dancing in equal parts. She and Alan got on like a house on fire.

'God, Alli,' said Tucker at one point. 'No wonder you slagged me off for asking if she was ugly. She's terrific. D'you think she'll date him? They might go out together.'

They were dancing around the living room, both with sausage rolls and drinks in either hand. Allison would not commit herself.

'I hope he's not going to bank on that,' she said. 'She took some persuading to come at all. I had to tell her it wasn't a set up. You'd have thought I was suggesting the white slave trade.'

'Yeah,' said Tucker. 'Well, it's not very normal these days, it is? Organising a Date for a Mate? We could start a service up. Make a fortune.'

Allison knew that Andrea would not be dating Alan again – not for a while at any rate. She was going off on holiday to Majorca the next night, and she'd told her not to tell. It was the only basis on which she'd finally said she'd come to the party. Fair enough, Allison supposed. But a pity.

Neither Allison nor Michelle was enjoying it all that much. Allison had seen Passmore again two nights before and she'd had a hard time of it. She was in a double bind, because she felt miserable with guilt at two-timing Tucker, but she was almost afraid to actually say no to Ralph. He'd given her the love bite on her neck the night Tucker had stood her up – not a gentle one but a hard, deliberate bite to mark her and embarrass her, and she'd been afraid

111

he would do some terrible thing the second time also. Allison was afraid of Passmore far more now than she had been before. She thought he might be mad.

There was a second part to her guilt, though. Because she admitted to herself that she'd gone with Passmore again for a reason. She'd fancied him. And if she didn't anymore – if – she was unsure about fancying anybody. When the music ended and Tucker tried to grab her and spirit her away to a dark and nesty corner, she resisted.

'I want food,' she said. 'And lots and lots of drink. It's a *party*, Tucker.'

'Yeah,' he said. 'But hell, Alli – oh. Yeah, let's have another drink.'

Michelle knew why Allison was wearing a polo neck sweater, because her brother had told her. She'd asked Allison point blank what was under it earlier, and Alli had said a sticking plaster. That was true – she showed her – but it was not all the truth, and Mish was worried. Her brother had been exultant about marking Allison, and exultant that she'd gone out with him.

'I've knocked one of them out of the fight,' he said. 'And that fairy you go with will be next.'

Michelle ran her hand almost wearily through Tommy's curls as they cuddled on the sofa. Was it worth the aggro, she wondered. Tommy was such a nice boy, but he was that – a boy. She sighed, her thoughts wandering to events at the factory where she worked. Tony was chatting her something fierce, every hour of every working day. He was nearly ten years older than Tommy, and he had a car. *He* was no boy.

But he had a wife as well, so that was that. No man was ever going to mess her about. He wasn't the only one, though. There was a lot of chatting went on, at work. Tons of it.

Tommy kissed her, and she kissed him back. She liked Tommy.

'Let's have a drink,' she said.

Whatever plans the boys had had, the party ended with them unconscious in a variety of beds and sleeping bags, and the girls elsewhere – most of them at home. In the morning, amid the normal, easy wreckage, there was one disaster. Some halfwit with an aerosol had written Arsenal Rules OK on the living room wall.

'Bloody Nora,' said Tucker through his hangover. 'What *can* we do with that?'

Alan ran a professional, if bleary, eye over it.

'Only one thing, my son,' he said. 'Two rolls of matching paper and a pot of paste. How long have we got?'

Tucker consulted the clock on the mantelpiece.

'About six hours if we're lucky.'

Which left Michelle and Allison to do the cleaning and the washing up.

'Typical,' said Allison.

'But it was worth it, though?' asked Tucker, anxiously. 'Wasn't it?'

They all agreed. They tiredly enthused.

Oh yeah. It had been great.

Chapter Fifteen

It was three days later that things started to fall apart, and once started they went with a bang.

Tommy walked into trouble first, and he did it almost literally. He was on his way to work, and as he turned the corner of a block of flats he met Passmore's fist. It was not a punch, it was just a fist, on the end of an outstretched arm. Tommy, who had not been concentrating, ended up on his backside. The jar to the base of his spine was almost as painful as his squashed nose.

Passmore was leering down at him.

'You should watch where you're going, Sunshine,' he said. 'Fancy a bit of toecap, do you?'

Tommy scarmbled to his feet as the big boot drew back. He leaned against a wall. A thick trickle of blood was running over his upper lip into his mouth.

'You twat,' he said. 'What did you do that for?'

He did not attempt to run, for two reasons. He expected he'd be caught, and he thought it was too early in the morning for a fight. He guessed this was a warning session. He was right.

'When will you take a hint, you jerk?' asked Passmore. 'I keep trying to tell you quite politely to lay off my sister, and what do you do?'

He moved forward, so Tommy moved away from the wall into more open ground. Passmore bunched his fist and waved it.

'I won't hit you now,' he said. 'Don't worry. In fact, if you do what I tell you, I might not hit you at all. Not ever again. All you've got to do is lay off my sister. I'll give you a written bleeding guarantee if you like.'

Tommy tried to look unconcerned. He didn't do too well. His face was hurting – and the expression on Passmore's frightened him.

'Why?' he said.

Passmore sighed.

'All right,' he said. 'If that's your attitude. I suppose it's better that way. No – don't jump like a bleeding rabbit. I won't do you today. Brains wants a go. We fancy working as a team on your alterations. We want to take our time.'

'Look, Passmore,' said Tommy. 'I don't know why you –'

'Oh shut your whining mouth,' said Passmore. 'Why can't you be sensible like your mate? Tucker took the hint. Why can't you?'

'You what? Tucker took what hint? What you talking about?'

Passmore's eyes narrowed.

'Him and Allison,' he said. 'Didn't he like to tell you, Sunshine? Or did he claim that neck-bite for himself? He hasn't got the bottle!'

'You're cracked,' said Tommy, bemused. 'She was at the party with him Friday. She was with him last . . .'

Passmore's face had changed. It had become thinner, full of tension.

'Oh was she now,' he breathed. 'Oh *was* she now . . .'

Tommy had a sinking feeling. Oh God. What *had* he done?

He began to edge away. But Passmore ignored him. He was holding his clenched fist in front of him. Staring at it.

Allison was on her way to school when Passmore reached her. He stepped out from behind a hedge on her route and stood in front of her. Involuntarily, Alli's hand flew to her throat. Her bite was still covered with a scarf.

'Yeah,' said Passmore, nastily. 'You hid it from Tucker all right, didn't you? I marked you up as mine and you hid it from him. You little slag.'

Allison licked her lips.

'I don't know what you're on about, Ralph,' she said. 'I couldn't go to school with a . . . lovebite . . . could I?'

Passmore reached for the scarf, but Allison jumped backwards. She was frightened.

'Look,' said Passmore. 'I'm not going to hurt you, Allison. I love you.'

115

'Why are you doing this, then, Ralph? Why are you terrorising me? Why don't you let me go to school?'

'I will.' He smiled at her, but it was a dangerous smile, an odd smile. Allison felt frightened to her stomach.

'Thank you,' she said. Almost a whisper. Ralph Passmore did not move. 'May I pass then, please? Ralph?'

'When you've answered me a question,' he replied. 'Have you been seeing Jenkins? Did you go to a party with him? Where were you last night?'

It was a big, wide street with trees. There were hardly any people about. What should she do? Tell the truth?

'No,' she said. 'It's not true, Ralph. I was at my cousin's on Friday. Andrea's. You can ask her if you like. And last night – '

Passmore moved in like a striking snake.

'Liar!'

Allison panicked completely. She threw her head backwards and screamed. Passmore made a grab at her, to shut her up. She broke away, still screaming.

'Allison! Shut up!'

His hand darted out, as she was turning to try and run. His knuckles smacked into her eye. Allison staggered, banging into a garden wall. She almost fell. She was crying, with pain and fear. But she had stopped screaming.

A couple of people were passing on the other side. They saw a small girl in school uniform cowering before a tall, powerful skinhead. They did not stop.

'Allison,' said Ralph Passmore. 'Oh Alli. I didn't mean to hurt you.'

Allison's eyes were blurred with tears.

'Well you did, you did,' she said. 'You cowardly great bastard. You hurt me!'

She pushed past and began to run.

'Allison!' he called. He made no move to stop her. 'Allison! Come back!'

She went on running. Ralph Passmore kicked a wall. Hard.

When Tommy arrived at the yard, full of fear at what he'd given away, and full of pain from his punched nose, he did

116

not even manage to get a word in – let alone be the main attraction. Tucker and Mr H were at the end of a row, and it had been a violent one. As Tommy came through the gate, he heard Tucker saying: 'Yeah, and this time I mean it. You can stick your bleeding pocket money right where you can find a small enough hole for it. I've had it up to here. I'm *not* your rotten slave.'

'It's a reasonable request,' said Mr Hargreaves. His face was red with anger. 'All I'm asking you to do is – '

'Break my back with lifting out a boiler, and work the extra for no extra pay. You're barmy, Mr Hargreaves. You're out of your box.'

'All right! Go then, you lazy little sod. Go! I don't want you in my yard no more if you're not prepared to work!'

They both noticed Tommy. Alan, who was standing a few feet back, had already given him a weak smile.

'Right,' said Tucker. 'Come on, Tom. We're finished here. He wants *more* work, now, for the same pay. I'm not taking it, and if you do, you're a fool.'

Mr Hargreaves shouted: 'Let him make his own mind up, you barrack room lawyer! Tommy, wait till I explain.'

But Tucker was pushing his bike out of the gate. Tommy shook his head at Mr H, avoiding his eye.

'Sorry,' he mumbled. 'Urgent business. Things to do. Tucker's my mate.'

As they left, Mr Hargreaves turned and roared at Alan.

'Go on then, you fat sod. I suppose you'll be going with them, won't you!'

Alan did not smile.

'I'll stay with you,' he said. 'Come on. Let's get started.'

Mr Hargreaves was silenced for a moment. But he was still aggressive.

'Why?' he demanded. 'You don't bloody want to. So why?'

Alan's reply was hardly audible.

'Because you're my bleeding *father*,' he said. 'Don't you know *anything*?'

Down the road, Tucker was steaming. Tommy could still not get a word in. He was calling Mr Hargreaves all kinds of miserable swine, and his son no better. He was glad, he said, that Alan had finally found the truth out about Andrea. He'd gone round her house at last because no one answered the phone. A neighbour had told him she was away on holiday. For three weeks. 'Women!' he said, with some sort of bitter satisfaction. So Tommy Watson dared not break *his* news.

'What's old Hargreaves after?' he asked. 'Why've we walked out? Jesus, Tucker, I don't half need the bread. Can we afford to?'

'He'll come round,' said Tucker. 'We've got him by the shorts. He's taken on another job and he wanted to take the plumber off the central heating work. The plumber he *said* he'd hire. He wanted us to get the boiler out, all on our tod. And do extra in the evenings "for a while". For a bleeding while, my arse! He'll come round. If we let him stew for a while, he'll come crying to us, cap in hand. He'll up the price.'

He did not sound very sure, and neither was Tommy. It sounded pretty damned unlikely to him.

'What about Alan, though?' he said. 'What sort of a mate's *he* turned out to be?'

But Tucker, on reflection, had changed sides, there.

'He hadn't got much choice, had he, though? It is his dad. Even if he *is* the meanest twat in London. It is his dad. Hey, Tom. What happened to your nose? Walk into the proverbial door, did you?'

Crunch time. Tommy coloured.

'Passmore,' he said.

'Oh God. Is the Incredible Hulk still out of his cage? I thought that'd all blown over. About Michelle, was it?'

'Yer.'

'Well come on,' said Tucker, after Tommy had left a meaningful pause. 'Spit it out. Is something biting you? As well as your usual fleas, of course,'

'Tuck,' said Tommy. 'Look, I. Look, I'm sorry but. Look, Passmore said something.'

Tucker felt a slight unease.

'About me, you mean? That he's going to duff me? You get used to it. I'll worry when it happens.'

118

Another pause.

'No,' said Tommy Watson. 'About Allison. He said. He said they're back together. He said he . . . bit her neck.'

On the outside, Tucker went white. The brown skin around his eyes suddenly stood out like a pair of goggles. Inside, he felt sick. He thought he might collapse. Oh shit, oh shit, he thought. No. Tell me it's not true. Tell me.

But he knew it was. He'd wondered about the plaster on her neck, and he'd wondered about her attitude, and he'd wondered about the fact she'd not come out a couple of times. But he'd convinced himself he ought to be ashamed. For not trusting her. He'd convinced himself.

'Tucker,' said Tommy.

'Piss off, Tom,' said Tucker. He switched on his ignition with a trembling hand.

'I'm sorry,' said Tommy.

'Just piss off, mate. All right? And . . . and thanks for telling me. I mean it.'

For a lot of that evening, Tucker tried to get in touch with Allison. He phoned several times, but was told she was not in. That hurt very badly, but he figured it could be true. He supposed she was out with Passmore.

Knowing it was foolish, and masochistic, and even dangerous, Tucker took his bike out and drove around the haunts. If he found them out together, what would he do? In waves of angry lunacy, he thought he'd kill the bitch. Then he'd be disgusted with himself. Yeah, he jeered. Because she's small, and weak. Why not think of killing Passmore? Because he'd slaughter you, that's why. You coward.

After about an hour, he spotted Passmore. And although he was not alone, he was not with Allison. He was with Brains and a couple of other big skins. Tucker felt rage and pain at the sight of him, but this time his excuse was watertight. Passmore he *might* dare to tackle alone. But there was little point in ending up as mincemeat.

Even if it would be one way out. Another stab of agony. Maybe not a bad way out, either. But he drove past, anonymous in the darkness and his helmet. Hating and hurting. Hating and hurting.

He phoned some more, and on the second time they just put the phone down. After her father's voice had said: 'She does not want to talk to you. She does not want to see you. She does not want you to ring her up. So cease.'

Later, he was lying on his bed in his room. With the light off. Alan came in and talked to him, although he told him to go away.

'Listen, Tucker,' Alan said. 'I know it's horrible. But you're not the only one. You heard about Andrea, I told you. But Tommy got the rush tonight.'

Jesus. Tucker did not speak, but he was interested.

'He phoned up Mish to ask about her brother and Alli and everything, and if it was all true and that. And she told him *they* were all over, as well. Just like that, out of the blue. She said she'd got another feller. At the cake factory. An older guy. With money. And a car.'

'Christ,' said Tucker. 'She always was a gold-digging little cow.'

'That's what Tommy said. But she said she wasn't. She said he was too young and that. She said it wasn't serious and he'd wake up in the morning and he wouldn't give a bugger. She said he was kidding himself, and we should all enjoy ourselves and not go on like Rudolph Valentino. She didn't sound upset at all, he said.'

Tucker thought about that. But he and Allison had been in love. It was different. He *was* in love.

'What do you reckon, Al? You've had a knockback with Andrea.'

Alan sighed.

'I don't mind that,' he said. 'She'll be coming home in a couple of weeks.'

He let out a laugh.

'She probably won't want to see me,' he added. 'But that don't seem to matter any more. I'm glad it happened, that's all. It was a great night, while it lasted. And . . . well – I can't be *that* repulsive, can I? Cause Andrea didn't think so, and she was fabulous.'

Tucker did not respond. He could get the drift. It may be all right for Alan, though, and even for Tommy, perhaps. But he . . . He was in love.

'I'm glad you can take it so light, Al,' he said. 'You're right, too. After Andrea you'll get others, you're bound to. She might even . . .'

He rolled over on his bed.

'Oh leave me alone, will you mate?' he said. 'I'm sorry, but . . . Just piss off, eh? Just leave me alone.'

Chapter Sixteen

Because he had no work to do, Tucker was able to continue his quest the next day. That's what it felt like. The lonely, lost traveller searching for the precious item, the thing that had been stolen from him.

He went to the school playground first, in break time. But it quickly turned out that Allison was not there. None of her friends knew why, she just had not turned up.

That made Tucker's heart soar, because it meant she would be at home. Her father would be at work, and presumably her mother. He kicked the bike into action and roared off round there. Feeling incredibly nervy, he parked it and walked up the garden path. Dingdong, went the chimes.

While he waited, Tucker rehearsed what he would say. Then he gave it up. The thought of Allison and Passmore. The lovebite on her neck. It was too much. He feared he might break down when she appeared, or something daft like that. He might weep or something criminal.

He was so lost in himself that he did not press the bell again for ages. He came to, realising he'd been standing there, doing nothing, like a dummy. But nobody had come. He pressed the chimes a second time. After a couple of minutes he gave up. She was not in.

She was, but she was not coming. As Tucker drove away, Allison pulled aside a net curtain in her bedroom and watched him go. She had a huge black eye.

It was dinnertime the day after that before he got to see her, or even to speak. Half a dozen phone calls that night, and a threat from Mr Powell that he would call the police. Then more calls in the morning, unanswered. Tucker had at last gone into the school and tried to get her out of her classroom with some ludicrous tale to the secretary that he was her cousin, and she had an appointment for a measles jab. That established one thing useful, though. She *was* there.

By midday, he had arrived back at the school, with his bike hidden down a side street, and himself well out of view. He wasn't crazy, after all. He may not be able to accept that his true-love did not love him, but he did realise that she was trying to avoid a meeting. If she knew he was out there lurking, she'd probably not emerge.

As it happened, he waited till almost half past before Allison appeared. He suspected that some girls had done recces for her. He'd seen two or three come out, and look around, then go back in again. Presumably Alli's spies.

When he saw her coming, Tucker ducked behind a garden hedge until she was on the road. Too late for her to dart back without running. Too late for her to escape without drawing attention to herself. He materialised beside her like a ghost.

'Alli!' His voice was horrified. 'What's happened to your face!'

She jumped a foot, and tried to get away. Tucker grabbed her wrist. Allison struggled for a moment, then gave up.

'Tucker,' she said. 'You shouldn't. It's over. You've got to leave me alone.'

'Your face,' he insisted. 'Who did that? Passmore?'

'It's none of your business. Let me go. I want to work. I want to be left alone. Stop bugging me. Stop picking on me. Leave me *alone*!'

She began to jerk, trying to break his hold. She looked pale, frightened, as if *he* was going to hit her. Some girls, walking past, faltered. They looked concerned.

'Tell them it's all right,' hissed Tucker. 'They think I'm attacking you.'

'You *are* attacking me! Oh Tucker, *please*. I can't stand it anymore. Leave me *alone*!'

Tucker knew he was defeated. There was going to be a scene, big trouble.

'Passmore?' he said. 'Alli. You've got to tell me. I know you've been with him. Did he do that?'

Allison was on the point of tears. She nodded.

'Right!' said Tucker. 'That's it then. I'll get the bastard!' He freed her wrist.

'No!' said Allison. 'No! Why must you all be so stupid? So ridiculous? Why must you all behave like mindless *morons* all the time?'

But Tucker had a real mission now. A real quest. One kind of pain was over, sunk in rage.

Another kind was coming up.

Tucker's search for Passmore was not a difficult one. It was a sunny day, and he ranged the streets on the bike like some strangely modern cowboy, in his black leather and black helmet, on his strangely modern horse. He saw Passmore sitting outside a pub with a pint of lager in his hand. He was with Brains.

Tucker drew to a halt and approached. He was very well aware already that this whole thing was ridiculous, some childish game with little basis in reality. But it suited him, for the moment. He remembered Alli's eye, and tried to recall the rage. He could recall how strong the rage had *been*, and that was enough. There were better things, after all, than the pangs of betrayal – easier things to bear. Both he and Passmore had this coming to them.

The challenge was made without fear, and accepted with pleasure and contempt. Passmore and Brains drained their glasses simultaneously.

'You're not allowed to wear your helmet,' said Brains. 'Clip it to your bike and leave them here. You may just be fit enough to ride when Passmore's done with you.'

'Yeah,' said Ralph. 'I'm feeling pretty generous today.'

They went to a nearby skating park, where a few small kids were messing about on the concrete. They stopped their wheeling when they saw what was happening, and gathered into groups, apprehensive yet excited. Passmore took his watch off, and placed it in his pork-pie hat. He gave them to Brains.

'Hang on to them, son,' he said. 'And try not to nick the watch, eh? It's a present from my tart.'

'Oh yeah, I know her, Chief,' said Brains. 'What's her name now? Allison Lovesit, ain't it?'

The fear that had been sapping Tucker was replaced by a flash of real anger. He rushed at Passmore, to a cheer from the crowd of small boys. He landed a blow to his nose, and other to his right ear. Passmore staggered back a pace or two.

'You bully, Passmore,' shouted Tucker. 'Hitting bloody gir – '

Passmore jumped forward like a man on a spring. Tucker's hands went up, but a fist came through and crunched into his forehead. The other one turned into a hand, that tore at his hair and ear. Tucker almost went down. He wobbled backwards, trying to keep his feet. Passmore let him get his balance. He did not bother to take the advantage.

'How long before they close?' he asked Brains. 'It's thirsty work, this. When you're as unfit as I am.'

The children laughed.

'Take your time, Boss,' said Brains. 'According to your watch there's a good two hours yet. And more.'

Tucker sprang, hoping to take Passmore off guard. No chance. As he flailed, Passmore broke through with both fists. The right squashed his nose, the left – turning into an open hand again – grabbed the flesh of his cheek and twisted.

Then Passmore got fed up with playing. He gave a grunt, and moved in. Blows rained on Tucker's face and head. Fingers gripped him underneath the chin. He was lifted, agonisingly, and thrown backwards on to the concrete, where he lay panting. There was blood on his face.

The small boys had gone quiet. Most of them were very frightened.

The first boot caught Tucker in the ribs, and that was bad enough. But Passmore had to pause there for a moment, because Tommy and Alan had arrived. Bringing up the rear, a hundred yards away, was Allison, who had found them in the chippy and told them what was up. Alan, panting and fat, barged into Passmore, knocking him off his feet. As Tucker tried to get up, Passmore grabbed Alan and pulled him down. Then he knelt on his stomach and bounced upright. He stamped on Alan's solar plexus with his heel to complete the job. That was Alan out.

Tommy tackled Brains, and Brains flattened him in a split second. The punch knocked Tommy flying and he

125

rolled into a dirty puddle. He did not get up for more. Before Tucker was half ready, Passmore smashed him in the face and kicked him in the stomach. When he was properly on the floor he prepared for a serious kicking session.

'Ralph!' screamed Allison. 'You sod! You sod! You sod!'

She was breathless, and half crying. She grabbed Passmore's arm and almost spat at him.

'You lousy *bully*, Ralph. Why can't you leave anyone *alone*!'

Passmore turned on her and raised his other fist like a hammer.

'Yes!' screamed Allison, hysterically. 'Go on, why *don't* you! You've done it before, you bastard! Why don't you do it again!'

Most of the little boys had gone. The last one or two were slinking away. Passmore dropped both his arms. He sneered at Allison.

'Oh piss off, Allison,' he said. 'You're such a drag, you middle class plonks. You're such a bleeding drag.'

He lounged across to Brains, who had not even dropped the hat and watch in dealing with Tommy Watson.

'Come on, Brains,' he said. 'Let's go and have a drink. While Florence Nightingale picks up the little pieces.'

Tucker, sitting up and bleeding quietly, said: 'You touch that motorbike, Passmore, and I'll call the police this time. I mean it.'

'My, you're not easy to teach, are you Tucker? What *would* I do to you, I wonder? But never mind, Sunshine. I'm not in the mood. Too much fun in one dinnertime can be a bind.'

The three of them formed a group. Allison stood in front. They watched Passmore and Brains walk off.

'Are you all right?' asked Allison.

'Yes,' said Tucker. 'Allison. I did it for you.'

'You needn't have bothered,' she replied. 'Don't you think I've had enough of fights, and thuggery, and stupid bloody boys who think they're hard men? I'm going back to school.'

There was no doubt in her voice. She meant it.

'Can I . . . Shall I . . .?'

'No,' she said. 'You can leave me alone. I'm sorry, Tucker, but I've had enough. I've had just about enough.'

Tucker and Tommy Watson were at the Dole House bright and early next day, expecting Alan to join them. They were in the queue for Box Six, waiting to be insulted by the beautiful Medusa. They'd been comparing injuries.

'God knows what would have happened if you lot hadn't come along,' said Tucker. 'How did you find me?'

'Luck mainly,' said Tommy. 'And . . . and Allison, of course. She rounded me and Alan up, then we tried the odd pub. We saw your bike outside the Waggon and guessed you'd gone to the skate place. Obvious.'

'It's a good job she cared *that* much,' said Tucker. 'Probably saved my looks, if not my life. You don't look bad with that split lip, as it happens.'

'Yeah.' Tommy grinned. 'I saw Mish this morning, early on. With a bloke. She looked quite interested in her brother's handiwork.'

'Jeez,' said Tucker. 'Did it hurt? Seeing her like that, I mean?'

'Not really,' replied Tommy. 'To be quite honest – I hardly felt a thing. Incredible. How about you and Alli? How does that fee – '

'Look, do me a favour, Tommy. Just leave it out, all right? Hey – there's big Alan.'

Big Alan was beaming. He hurried up to them. He flashed a look at Medusa.

'Lose your places in the queue lads, this is important,' he hissed.

'Sod off, Al! You must be joking!'

'All right then, but don't go crazy when I tell you this. Listen. Tucker! Get your head close.'

They went into a huddle. They could smell the coffee and baked beans on Alan's breath.

'Three guesses.'

'For pox sake, Al!' whispered Tucker. 'Tell us before I break your crummy neck.'

'Me dad! He's given in. He wants you back, desperate. He's offering another two quid each. A week!'

Tommy almost blew it. They had to hold him down and clamp his mouth up.

'Two quid!' breathed Tucker. 'Each! Hey, Al, that's superb. I told you, Watson, oh ye of little faith! I told you so! This calls for a drink. A big one!'

'Yeah,' said Alan. 'But he needs us today. All of us. We've got to start this afternoon.'

Tommy Watson and Tucker Jenkins laughed out loud. Medusa glanced at them sharply. Happiness was frowned on in Dole House. Everything was, except servility.

'He's got no chance,' said Tucker. 'Today we celebrate!'

'That's what I thought you'd say,' said Alan. 'So I chanced me arm. I went insane. You see those three over there? On that bench by the door? I've asked them for a drink.'

They could not credit it. They looked at Alan, then they clocked the girls. They were new ones. At least, they were not recognised.

'You old villain!' said Tommy. 'You dirty little dog!'

'Well,' said Alan, modestly. 'They're only young. First-timers. They were very easy to impress for an old hand like me.'

The girls were parked demurely on the black plastic seat. They smiled shyly, then giggled, when they saw they were being watched.

Tucker felt quite odd. Exhilarated. One of them looked just his type. Delicious.

'Hey,' he said. 'Before I agree to this rash step, Al, there's one thing I want to know.'

'What's that, my son?'

'Have any of them got a brother? Because if they *have*, mate – you can bloody well forget it!'

'Mr Jenkins,' said Medusa. 'I am waiting. And will you please cut out the foul language.'

'Yes, ma'am,' said Tucker Jenkins. 'Give us a big wet kiss!'